ABOUT THE AUTHOR

George G. Gilman was born in 1936 in what was then a small village east of London. He attended local schools until the age of fifteen. Upon leaving school he abandoned all earlier ambitions and decided to become a professional writer, with strong leanings towards the mystery novel. He wrote short stories and books during evenings, lunch hours, at weekends, and on the time of various employers while he worked for an international newsagency, a film company, a weekly book-trade magazine and the Royal Air Force.

His first short (love) story was published when he was sixteen and the first (mystery) novel ten years later. He has been a full-time writer since 1970, writing mostly Westerns which have been translated into a dozen languages and have sold in excess of 16 million copies. He is married and lives on the Dorset coast, which is as far west as he intends to move right now.

The STEELE series by George G. Gilman
and published by New English Library:

ADAM STEELE 1: THE VIOLENT PEACE
ADAM STEELE 2: BOUNTY HUNTER
ADAM STEELE 3: HELL'S JUNCTION
ADAM STEELE 4: VALLEY OF BLOOD
ADAM STEELE 5: GUN RUN
ADAM STEELE 6: THE KILLING ART
ADAM STEELE 7: CROSS-FIRE
ADAM STEELE 8: COMMANCHE CARNAGE
ADAM STEELE 9: BADGE IN THE DUST
ADAM STEELE 10: THE LOSERS
ADAM STEELE 11: LYNCH TOWN
ADAM STEELE 12: DEATH TRAIL
ADAM STEELE 13: BLOODY BORDER
ADAM STEELE 14: DELTA DUEL
ADAM STEELE 15: RIVER OF DEATH
ADAM STEELE 16: NIGHTMARE AT NOON
ADAM STEELE 17: SATAN'S DAUGHTER
ADAM STEELE 18: THE HARD WAY
ADAM STEELE 19: THE TARNISHED STAR
ADAM STEELE 20: WANTED FOR MURDER
ADAM STEELE 21: WAGONS EAST
ADAM STEELE 22: THE BIG GAME
ADAM STEELE 23: FORT DESPAIR
ADAM STEELE 24: MANHUNT
ADAM STEELE 25: STEELE'S WAR: THE WOMAN
ADAM STEELE 26: STEELE'S WAR: THE PREACHER
ADAM STEELE 27: STEELE'S WAR: THE STOREKEEPER
ADAM STEELE 28: STEELE'S WAR: THE STRANGER
ADAM STEELE 30: THE KILLER MOUNTAINS
ADAM STEELE 31: THE CHEATERS
ADAM STEELE 32: THE WRONG MAN
ADAM STEELE 33: THE VALLEY OF THE SHADOW
ADAM STEELE 34: THE RUNAWAY
ADAM STEELE 35: STRANGER IN A STRANGE TOWN
ADAM STEELE 36: THE HELLRAISERS
ADAM STEELE 37: CANYON OF DEATH
ADAM STEELE 38: HIGH STAKES
ADAM STEELE 39: ROUGH JUSTICE
ADAM STEELE 40: THE SUNSET RIDE
ADAM STEELE 41: THE KILLING STRAIN
ADAM STEELE 42: THE BIG GUNFIGHT
ADAM STEELE 43: THE HUNTED

CODE OF THE WEST

George G. Gilman

NEW ENGLISH LIBRARY
Hodder and Stoughton

for
JERRY
Son of the sheriff!

A New English Library Original Publication

First New English Library Paperback Edition 1987

British Library Cataloguing in Publication Data

Gilman, George G.
Code of the west.—(Adam Steele; 44)
Rn. Terry Harknett I. Title II. Series
823'.914[F] PR6058.A686/

ISBN 0-450-41203-2

The characters and situations in this book are entirely imaginary and bear no relation to any real person or actual happening

Printed and bound in Great Britain for Hodder and Stoughton Paperbacks, a division of Hodder and Stoughton Ltd., Mill Road, Dunton Green, Sevenoaks, Kent (Editorial Office: 47 Bedford Square, London, WC1 3DP) by Cox & Wyman, Reading, Berks.

1

It was the winter time of the year, but Adam Steele was as grateful as ever to the destiny that had steered him to this piece of California and allowed him to put down roots here. For the seasonal variations that came to the Providence River Valley which cut through the lower western foothills of the Sierra Nevadas were much to his taste.

It was good, after a long and not overly hot summer, to see the colours of the landscape gradually change through fall. Then to feel the crystal clear air get chillier and damper as the winter, never too cold or too wet, set in. For just long enough so that, come March, he looked eagerly forward to the onset of spring.

He had spent too long in parts of the country where it was always too hot or too cold all the time, or where little about the terrain changed with the seasons: while he searched for the ideal stretch of land to settle down in, to end his drifting existence.

Or, probably, it had only seemed that way. For had he ever stayed in one place long enough for anything ordered by nature to change, after circumstances forced him to abandon his Virginia birthright so long ago? If so, was there ever an inclination to pause and look around, to note what was happening on all sides of him: except to seek out the first sign of danger before it struck, and to . . .

Steele abruptly interrupted this line of thought with a grunt, guessed the look on his freshly shaved face was as sour as the sound to his own ears. Then he made a conscious effort, drew back his lips and crinkled his eyes into some kind of a smile. Which, because it was not spontaneous, he knew, lacked the genuine warmth that would have been in his expression when he first began to relish satisfaction with his circumstances a few minutes ago. Gave free rein to his contented mind when he remounted his gelding after he had closed and fastened the gate across the spur trail at the entrance of the Trail's End spread.

Recommenced to ride the spur across the thickly timbered plateau beside the slow-trickling Timber Creek. Next started down the gentle slope of the fir-covered hill to where the spur intersected the main Providence to Broadwater trail after it forded the Providence River near where the creek joined it.

It was as his horse splashed through the shallow water that his mind began to unearth unwelcome memories of times long ago which he had lately found it easier to keep buried.

Now he turned the gelding to the right, on to the trail that cut away from the curve of the river, to begin a winding course through the mixed timber to the town of Providence, a half mile to the south. And the manufactured smile began to sit more naturally on his face after he saw the poles spaced along the eastern side of the trail had been strung with telegraph wire since he was last by this way. That this sign of yet another incursion of the outside world into his life should trigger pleasure was a measure of just how happy was Adam Steele with his lot.

He was a man closer to fifty than forty, who could unintentionally look many years younger at first impression: if he happened to be displaying a boyish grin of good humour rather than a quiet smile of satisfaction. But mostly he looked his true age: this not entirely due to the colour of his hair, which had prematurely whitened when he was a young man and nowadays showed hardly a trace of the flame red it had been during his youth.

Beyond a first impression that invariably centred upon the white hair, worn neatly trimmed but with long sideburns, an observer would note the lines inscribed into the element-burnished skin of his face. The worldly, slightly world-weary look in his coal black eyes was additional evidence that here was a man approaching a half century of years. And the more perceptive observer might realise that not all those years had been filled with the contentment he experienced this bright, chill mid-morning of a newly started year.

At first glance, also, a casual observer might consider this slow-riding man incapable of achieving what those who knew him were aware he had attained: in the bad old days and during the more recent, mostly good ones. For his height was just a little over five and a half feet and his frame leaned toward the wiry rather than the muscular. And when he was attired as he was today, he certainly looked more the privileged son of a rich Easterner than the quick-to-kill saddletramp he became before he settled at Trail's End and changed it from an abandoned, derelict spread into a fine and profitable horse ranch.

Today he was riding to town to transact some bank business: make to Ethan Brady another repayment of the loan the banker had granted him to stock the spread with breeding animals. And whenever Adam Steele had business of this nature in town, he chose to garb himself in the kind of clothing he had once worn most of the time. The kind that had caused him often to be scorned as a dude in the bad old days.

Back then, his style of living hard, sleeping beside as well as riding along the open trails more often than not, had seldom allowed him to keep such an outfit as neat and clean as he would have wanted for very long. Not like now: when the cream-coloured suit he wore this January morning, along with the pale blue vest, white satin shirt and highly polished black riding boots, all were much as they had been when he first took them out of the packages in which they had been dispatched from the mail order house in Chicago. For this was only the third occasion on which he had donned the clothing. And on the other times he had carefully stored the clothes away when he got back home from town.

This idiosyncratic style of dress on infrequent special occasions was one of the few material straws he consciously clung to of how things had been when he enjoyed the wealth and privileges of being heir to one of the largest plantations in Virginia: before the War Between the States brought that way of life to such an explosive, tragic end.

At odds with the immaculate stylishness of the city suit was a pair of black, scuffed buckskin gloves, a worse-for-wear low crowned, flat-brimmed Stetson, also black, and a well-worn grey kerchief. The hat he liked to wear at all times, the gloves comprised of a kind of good luck charm and the kerchief was actually an Oriental weapon of strangulation. These items had their origins in his days as a drifter wanted for murder, heading for nowhere until the seed of an idea for something like Trail's End was sown in his mind.

Also striking an odd note compared with the neatness of the hardly worn suit was that the outside seam of his right pants leg was split for a few inches, midway between the knee and the cuff. This was not a fault in the manufacture of the pants: but a purposely made slit, through which Steele could reach and draw a finely balanced throwing knife carried in a boot sheath.

Both the thuggee scarf and the wood-handled knife were replacements for the original weapons he acquired in more dangerous times. Unlike the rifle that jutted from the forward-hung boot on the right side of his saddle. An old and unusual weapon: a Colt Hartford six shot revolver action rifle with a fire-scorched rosewood stock to the right side of which was screwed a small gold plate inscribed: *To Benjamin P. Steele, with gratitude—Abraham Lincoln.*

Absently, as he started along the curve of the trail and entered the trees, losing sight of the Providence River, Steele reached out a gloved hand and ran a forefinger over the metal plate.

Then he heard a gust of boisterous laughter, not far ahead of him in the timber. A sound which made a not unpleasant incursion against the surrounding stillness disturbed until then only by the clop of the gelding's hooves, the rippling of running water and the calls of birds which, like Steele, were happy to remain in this neck of the woods for the winter instead of taking off for warmer climes.

This rifle, although acquired in violent circumstances, was another material link with the best of the good days: his sole inheritance from Ben Steele who, had not the war left it in ruins would have passed on the plantation and all it meant in terms of rich, easy living.

The Colt Hartford, and the clothing he wore today, were links with the past he was reluctant to sever: maybe the last ones. Even while he relished a life he had never thought he could accept so readily: when he had been seeking a place, as far removed from his fellow human beings as possible, irrespective of seasonal changes and much else. Just so long as he could spend the days raising fine horseflesh and the night sleeping in his own bed under his own roof. Without need of contact with a world in which, it had seemed often then, every man and woman, and every child even was intent upon harming him, or was determined to accidentally trigger a chain reaction which would culminate with harm to him.

He had needed to compromise on such a state of perfection, because the Trail's End spread was just too good an opportunity to pass up. Even if it was within less than a mile of Providence. A town populated by all kinds of people, none of whom meant him any real harm.

But a town into which strangers occasionally came. And caused trouble. Which, because of the kind of man he had been, Steele got involved in. Perhaps, then, he had not really changed.

Even though he was a horse rancher, starting to make a success of his business, able to acknowledge that the town offered him facilities which made the running of his business easier. And now, as he saw how close to completion was the telegraph line between Providence and Broadwater—and through Broadwater to the rest of California and beyond—he allowed that his life was likely to be made even easier.

'Davy, you sure are bound to break a lotta gals' hearts, is my opinion!' a man's voice cut in on Adam Steele's new train of thought.

'The hell with their hearts, kid!' another man added. 'It's a whole lot of maidenheads you'll be breakin', if you play your cards right!'

This triggered a fresh burst of laughter, ended when a younger sounding voice protested:

'Aw, quit it, why don't you!'

Somebody else growled earnestly: 'Yeah, cut it out, you guys. You're makin' the kid blush redder than an Arizona sunset.'

'Hell, that's all part of the first flush of youth, Jethro!' it was argued. 'It's my guess we're all green with envy Davy still has it and we sure enough don't.'

'That's damn right, Ryan,' a fifth member of the good-humoured bunch agreed. 'And we got regrets, too, I reckon. Regrets we didn't take advantage of all them sweet opportunities Davy Clavell's got ahead of him!'

'You speak for yourself, Coggins,' Jethro countered. 'I sure enough didn't allow too many of them kinda chances to pass me by when I was younger... Howdy, stranger.'

The greeting was addressed to Steele as he rode onto a straightaway of the trail through the timber, came into sight of the group of five men taking a smoke break from their morning's work. Sat on or leaned against a flatbed wagon with two horses in the traces which was parked near the latest pole to be strung with the telegraph line from Broadwater. Ample wire to complete the final link with Providence was wound around a spool on a winch fixed to the wagon bed.

'How are you fellers doing?' Steele responded as he rode closer to the group.

From long experience he was unperturbed at the way the four men and a boy of sixteen or so eyed him with curiosity, intrigued by the incongruity of his city-style outfit in these rural surroundings.

'Just fine, just fine,' the man whose voice identified him as Jethro answered as Steele halted his horse alongside the wagon.

At close to sixty, Jethro was the oldest of the bunch. The shortest and fattest, too: his squat frame topped by a round head that was almost hairless. A grin fitted readily on his ruddy complexioned features, and it mattered not he had so few teeth in gums clamped to the stem of a large-bowled pipe.

'Now there's a guy who knows how to catch the eyes of the ladies after that first flush of youth is long gone.'

Just as Steele recognised Jethro from his voice, so now he knew this far more harsh-toned speaker was Ryan. He was around forty, tall and broad-shouldered, with a muscular build and an aggressively featured face scarred by a bad complexion as well as age lines. There was a hint of scorn in his dark eyes, a match for his tone, as he tried to hold the Virginian's gaze for longer than Steele was prepared to allow. A fat cigar bobbed at the side of his mouth as he spoke.

'We was just ribbin' young Davy here about how a good lookin' boy like him won't have no trouble makin' it with the girls,' another man put in hurriedly. With a rebuking glare at Ryan.

This was Coggins. Of an age with Ryan, a half a head shorter and fifty pounds lighter. With an emaciated face to match his skinny frame. His features were dominated by a disproportionately large and bushy grey moustache.

'I heard,' Steele said evenly as he grinned at the still blushing youngster, added: 'Reckon I have to agree with them.'

Davy Clavell, rolling a cigarette, maybe was making a hash of it because his mind was on embarrassing other things. Or simply from inexperience. He was stockily built and had a finely chiselled, evenly tanned face from which clear blue eyes looked without a trace of hardness. His hair was not too blond nor too curly. His looks were sure to improve as he got older and the callowness of youth was matured out of his face.

'Shit!' he snarled as the paper disintegrated in his sweat-sticky fingers. He mangled it with the tobacco, hurled the whole mess away, glared at Steele then around at the others to growl: 'I don't give a damn what you or these guys think about the way I look! And gettin' girls ain't somethin' I need advice on from any of you!'

'Yeah, Davy,' the final member of the group said with a knowing grin and a wink. 'I heard there's a young lady in Providence already smitten with you. Ain't it that little girl from out——'

'Shut up, Jack!' the youngster cut in vehemently. 'Just shut the hell up!'

Jack looked like he could be Jethro's brother, younger than the bald man by ten years or so. He had much the same barrel-shaped body, round head and dark eyes crowded by fleshy lids. But he still had a full head of greying black hair and the hands with which he completed the rolling of a cigarette were strangely delicate for a fat man, compared with Jethro's pudgy ones. He was already smoking and now he extended the freshly-made cigarette toward Clavell.

'Stick it up your ass and give your brains a smoke!' the youngster snapped, once again seeming to draw confidence from profanity.

Jack shrugged and lodged the new cigarette behind an ear. Said to the mounted man on the other side of the wagon: 'Guess you're Steele? Guy that has the place at the end of the spur that cuts off west, short ways back up the trail?'

'You got it, feller.'

'Figured you couldn't have rode far. Lookin' the way you do. All neat and clean. Heard tell of you since we been stayin' in Providence.'

All five telegraph company men were attired in heavy duty work clothes that had not been laundered or darned in a long time: maybe since they had started in to dig the holes and raise the poles to carry the line from Broadwater to Providence.

'Reckon a lot of what you heard wasn't good?' Steele said without rancour.

Jack extended his right hand and rocked it gently from side to side as he once more shrugged his fleshy shoulders. 'Folks have all kinds of different views, Steele. It takes all kinds to make a world.'

'And in the world there's a whole lot of women just waitin' to be *made*, Davy!' Ryan said. Vented a raucous laugh as he dropped his cigarette butt, crushed it out under a boot heel.

'Hey, I figure we talked through that subject enough,' Jack said sourly, and it was now clear he was the top hand of the bunch. 'About time we got back to work, anyways. Before Steele here tells the local folks we're goofin' off on the job of bringin' the telegraph to town.'

He grinned to emphasise he was only joking. And Steele tipped his hat, responded with an easy grin of his own as he heeled his horse slowly forward:

'Unless I have something important to tell them. I never say much of anything to anybody.'

'That's a fine rule to have, mister,' Davy Clavell growled as he climbed up on to the back of the wagon, to stand beside the winch. 'I just wish these guys would keep their mouths shut until they had somethin' to say!'

'There's a more important rule you should be concerned with at your age, kid,' Ryan muttered with a grin. 'Part of the code of the west. A man's gotta do what a man's gotta do . . . And most women are mighty grateful about that!' His grin expanded into another harsh burst of laughter. Which he curtailed to call after Steele: 'Ain't that right, dude?'

The Virginian's initial dislike for Ryan was strengthened. So he had to manufacture another smile that failed to generate warmth in his coal black eyes as he looked back over his shoulder at the group dispersing from the wagon. Replied: 'Seems to me fellers who work for the telegraph company ought to know more than I do about codes. But I thought that part of it ran more like a man's got to screw what a woman's got to screw.'

2

It was not simply his ill feeling for one of the telegraph company work crew that discoloured Steele's mood as he completed his ride into Providence. Of greater influence was the way in which the naivete of Davy Clavell reminded him of the darkest cloud that had recently cast such a grim shadow across the happy state of affairs at Trail's End: the killing of Billy Baxter.

One of that handful of people from town who had accepted him for what he was virtually at first meeting, Billy was a man in his thirties with the physical strength of all those hard working years, but with the mental capabilities of a child of no more than six or seven.

There was no good reason why Billy should have died the way he did. But then that was the way things happened so often to people who came to mean something special to Adam Steele over the years. Now the mourning for Billy was done and the Virginian seldom thought of the man with the child's mind anymore. Except when he happened to catch sight of the grave, out back of the Trail's End house, on the bank of Timber Creek. Where Billy at last had perfect peace on the place that had been his only true home in boyhood and the latter days of his life.

Then Steele put all such morose thoughts out of his mind when he detected the first traces of woodsmoke on the pine-scented air. Which, had he not been familiar with the area, would have signalled that a town was close by; that fires, kept burning against the chill of the winter air, were now being stoked to greater heat to cook midday meals on many stoves throughout Providence.

A town of unusual layout, comprised of a square at this north side, with a short, conventional street at the south. Linking the two was a mile-long street that wound, trail-like through an extensive stand of timber. Occasional houses were sited along this winding thoroughfare, which was intersected here and there by spurs which led out to scattered farmsteads and ranches.

The first sight of town from the north was the rear of the law office and lock-up to the left at the end of the trail from Broadwater, and of the meeting hall to the right. The hall had a sign on the rear wall which Steele no longer felt was ironic when he applied its sentiment to himself. For he usually felt, of late, he was 'Welcome to Providence'.

The square on to which he emerged from between these two buildings was lined on the north and to the west and east with business and public premises, and on the south was enclosed by timber. As usual, it was quiet, calmly busy with merchants and citizens going about their own business of country town living.

After he had turned his mount to the left. Steele leaned down and glanced, almost involuntarily, through the window of the granite built law office. Saw that although the stove chimney gave off wisps of smoke the sheriff was not behind his desk.

Of all those people who, at the start, made known their antipathy toward the ex-drifter many suspected of being a gunslinger, Len Fallows had with good reason been the most vocal. But lately, after a lengthy period of untroubled time in the Providence River Valley, the lawman had mellowed in his attitude towards the Virginian. They were far from being friends but at least Fallows was not averse to exchanges of tersely polite greetings these days.

The lock-up beyond the barred, unglazed window was as empty as usual: Providence was a law-abiding town.

The neighbouring building, which housed the office and press room of the *Providence Post-Despatch*, was quiet. Probably it was deserted, as it inevitably was except for

Wednesdays and Thursdays. Huey Attrill, who ran his newspaper single handed, published every Thursday morning.

There was an unobtrusive buzz of talk interspersed with some clinking of glass against glass from beyond the batwinged entrance of Harry Krim's Golden Gate Saloon.

And from the stage line depot which with the saloon formed the north east corner of the square came the sound of Joanna Morrison singing; unmelodiously but happily. The woman, Steele guessed, was doubtless relishing the prospect of the extra income she and Michael, her son, would earn from having the telegraph office operating within her building: the San Francisco and Central California Stage Line Company sent a Concord down to Providence just once every four or five weeks.

Steele dismounted out front of the Golden Gate, which had the only hitching rail on this side of the square. The fact there were no other animals already tied there suggested it was a group of local businessmen from around the square who contributed to the rumble of talk in the saloon. Probably much the usual crowd for this time of day.

Harlan Grout, who operated the livery, would be among the morning drinkers. And most likely a couple of the storekeepers whose premises lined the west side of the square. Tom Knight, also, if he had been able to escape the eagle eye and slip the tight rein of his wife, Blanche, the prime mover in running the two-story boarding house beyond the livery.

Not Ethan Brady, though: he took his business as a banker very seriously. And so it proved, for the door of the First Providence Town Bank sited between the stage depot and the livery swung open at a touch. The banker greeted the Virginian brightly as he stepped over the threshold:

'Morning to you, sir. And a fine one it is, too. For this time of the year.'

Brady was on the brink of sixty. A short, flabby man with the pale face of one who spent much more time indoors than out. His sparse slicked-down grey hair was clipped too short, and his pale grey eyes seemed capable of conveying just two emotions: anxiety and avariciousness.

This morning, although his small mouth was shaped by a broad smile, the brightness of his eyes gleamed more with greed than simple good humour. Obviously he knew from Steele's mode of dress that the Virginian was here either to make a repayment against the existing loan or to negotiate a new one. And Brady was acquisitively happy to handle either kind of business for this customer.

He was himself attired in a shabby, shiny, city suit of sombre hue. Seated at the centre of the counter, with a grille to the ceiling above it, which divided the bank's main room into two. This morning he was feeling good enough not to indulge in a customary nervous habit of mopping non-existent sweat off his pasty, fat face.

'Weather's fine, feller. And me being able to pay you back another hundred dollars makes it an even better day.'

'Real good, real good. So things are still on the up and up at Trail's End, uh?'

Brady rose from his stool at the counter, turned and went through a doorway which gave on to a back room. Where he was out of sight for a few moments, delving into the safe in his private office.

Steele crossed the bare floor of the undecorated room, halted at the counter. Drew a wad of soiled and torn bills of various denominations from a hip pocket.

He called to Brady: 'Right. Sold a pair of foals to a Broadwater couple last week.'

'That's good, real good.'

'The money's a little the worse for wear,' Steele said to Brady as the banker emerged from the back room with a large ledger. 'Couple who bought the fillies for their daughters had been saving up a long time.'

Brady shook his head, eyes even brighter though he was no longer smiling so broadly. He set down the ledger and opened it at a place marked by his thumb as he replied; 'Honest dirt on honestly earned money is no cause for me to complain, Mr Steele. Only pity is, lots of savers keep their cash at the house instead of a bank. Give it here.'

Steele pushed the bills across the counter, through the gap beneath the grille. Felt no sense of ill-will as he watched the little fat man carefully count the money. Then Brady opened a drawer, took out a pen and an inkwell, made some entries in the ledger. He swung the book around so Steele could see that the hundred dollars had been deducted from the last entry on a page with his name at the top. Interest and capital repayments were listed in separate columns and Steele was able to see he still owed Ethan Brady sixteen hundred and twenty five dollars.

'Grateful to you.'

'And I to you, sir,' Brady replied absently, holding up the ledger and tilting it to check the ink was dry before he closed the book. 'I only wish certain other clients were so businesslike in their dealings with the bank.'

Steele nodded, turned and started for the door. Paused to look back when Brady said earnestly:

'I don't suppose you've heard anything that promises to put Trail's End on a sound business footing for you?'

'No, Mr Brady,' Steele said tightly. 'I told you: if I do, you'll be one of the first to know.'

The banker mopped at his face with the back of a hand as he answered: 'Yes, of course you did. I'm sorry to bring it up again.'

Steele shrugged and growled: 'I think about it more often than when you bring it up, feller.'

He continued to the door. Swung it inwards and stepped out of the shaded bank into the narrow strip of shadow cast by the building at near noon. Made an effort to put out of his mind the nagging anxiety Brady's comment had triggered.

This was the fact he had no legal title to Trail's End, which many local people continued to call 'the old Sanderson place'. For the house and barn were built and the rich land had first been worked by a family named Sanderson. Who had abruptly deserted the area one day, leaving the buildings to decay and the land to go to waste. They had paid no money for the three and a half thousand acres, but the spread had surely been theirs by right of settling it.

Not so very long ago, the insecurity of his tenure at Trail's End had been grimly highlighted. When a woman who claimed to be the sole heir of the true owners arrived in town while Steele was absent. She proved to be a crooked opportunist but one day a genuine claimant could appear on the scene, and what then...?

As always when this doubt crowded to the front of his mind, Steele was not easily able to relegate it to the back. Even though he was well practised in such mental exercises. For in the old days he had never burdened himself with concerns about what might happen in the future. But that was probably because in those times he had not had any kind of future worth worrying about?

'Good day to you, Mr Steele sir,' a woman's voice greeted cheerfully, to break in on his dark train of thought.

'And to you, Arlene,' he responded as the short and heavily built black woman of over sixty bustled on by, toting a box of cleaning materials. On her way from helping Blanche Knight with the chores at the boarding house to take care of similar work at either the law office or the meeting hall.

As usual, her round and shiny, jet black face was wreathed with a broad smile to convey her enjoyment of a life that lacked a great deal but also gave her much for which she was grateful.

Since Billy Baxter was killed, Arlene Forrester provided the only help Steele had out at Trail's End. She came to the place three times a week to clean, launder and cook for him.

'Be seein' you first thing tomorrow, uh?' she called back as she went on her way, as ever in a hurry to get her work done each day bar Sunday.

'Certainly hope so, Arlene,' Steele replied absently as the clock in the stage depot began to chime the hour of midday.

Then from within the schoolhouse beyond the meeting hall at the north west corner of the square Lavinia Attwood rang the hand bell to signal the end of morning lessons. Moments later the door opened and a host of chattering and laughing children spilled out on to the yard and across it to the gateway in the stone boundary wall: the youngsters relishing freedom after confinement in the single classroom for so long.

Steele kept in place the smile he had directed toward Arlene, as he relished his own sense of freedom: his independence within a community where all he owed was money to the banker and polite responses to those of his fellow citizens who chose to greet him.

Then he made to move toward the Golden Gate, as yet unsure whether he would step through the batwings to have a cup of coffee or swing up into his saddle to ride right on back to Trail's End. But he paused as a sound of galloping hoofbeats reached into the square. The horse being ridden at top speed over the final stretch of Main Street that opened out from the timber on the southside.

In a town like Providence, where the pace of daily life was invariably slow, the pounding of galloping hooves was cause for concern. And even the boisterous schoolchildren were affected into silence by the tension of their elders who emerged at many doorways to peer anxiously toward the gap in the timber from which the rider in a hurry would appear.

Then, just for a moment, Steele's attention was distracted from this focal point of mass interest by the sound of the bank door as it was opened. The rider galloped into sight and Ethan Brady said while he mopped at his brow with a handkerchief:

'What's Arnie Taggart in such a darn hurry for?'

Steele knew Taggart was a small scale rancher who ran a few head of cattle on a place to the east of Providence. A widower with a pretty young daughter some said he worshipped to an unhealthy extent. The Virginian had seen the man a few times before, when both Taggart and he happened to come to town on the same day to purchase supplies. Remembered him as a beefily built, strong-looking man of about forty with a ruggedly handsome face who was not much of a talker. It was said Taggart seldom spoke a word unless a curt nod or shake of his head failed to convey his meaning.

Some considered him surly. Others thought his taciturn attitude caused by shyness. He was vocally forthcoming today, though, after he brought his sweat-lathered gelding to a rearing halt on the centre of the square. Glowered around at each open doorway, roared:

'Where's Kate? Anyone here seen my Kate?'

A brief stillness was clamped down on all sides of the

mounted man in the wake of his dramatic arrival and thunderous demand. And at the centre of the inert silence, the heavy breathing of his horse sounded very loud: the rapid wrenching of the man's head from side to side appeared even more emphatic than it probably was.

'Answer me, one of you!' he snarled insistently. And rage with the lack of instant response transcended the deep concern responsible for his headlong haste and imperious commands.

From the gateway of the schoolyard the tall and thin Miss Attwood started to tell him in her well modulated voice: 'For one, I have certainly not seen your daughter. And——'

'Anyone seen my Kate?' Arnie Taggart cut in. Made a dismissive hand gesture in response to the schoolteacher's negative answer.

'Taggart!' Len Fallows barked. The harshness of the sheriff's tone was a match for that of the rancher. And everyone swept their gaze toward the saloon as he pushed out through the batwings. A tall, lean, fifty some man with a sun-burnished, rough-hewn face dominated by dark eyes and a thick black moustache. He was as neatly garbed as his wife always sought to make him.

'You seen her?' Taggart countered, jerked over on his reins to turn the gelding toward the Golden Gate. 'You seen my Kate? With that evil minded kid who works——'

Fallows strode purposefully away from the saloon entrance. And Grout, Knight, Attrill, Roland Decker the local butcher and Harry Krim himself jostled each other for the best advantage points in the doorway.

The lawman bellowed: 'No, I haven't seen your girl, Taggart! With anybody! In days! And I figure if anyone else had, they'd have answered you by now!' He moderated his tone and slowed his pace. 'Why don't you get down off your horse and step into my office? And we'll talk it over, find out if there's any cause for concern——'

'Cause for concern, damnit! I'll say there's cause for concern! That child of mine is likely with that lousy rotten kid now. Doin' things no girl of fifteen should ever——'

'You quit that kind of talk, Taggart!' Fallows roared, his

face reddening under its tan. 'There are women and children listening and——'

'You think I give a damn about somethin' like that when my little girl could right now be...'

He left it unfinished, but not out of feeling for the sensibilities of women and children. Cocked his head to one side in a listening attitude. And everyone now heard that the surrounding silence was kept from being absolute by the sound of more hooves. These approaching the square on the north trail. Two horses, moving without haste, hauling a clattering wagon.

All attention was directed toward the gap between the meeting hall and the law office. Taggart, sitting his horse on the centre of the square, was best positioned to first see and recognise the wagon and the men aboard it. Reacted by dropping a hand away from his reins to drape it over the butt of a revolver that jutted out of a holster, rucking up the bottom of his sheepskin coat.

'Oh, my God!' Ethan Brady gasped, hurriedly withdrew across the threshold of his bank. And closed the door to a crack through which he peered with one eye.

There was a muttering of talk from around the three building-lined sides of the square. A sudden stir of hurried activity. As people muttered much the same exclamations as Brady and many instinctively backed off a pace or two in token retreat. But no other doors were closed.

'Hold it, Taggart!' Len Fallows roared. Drew all attention except for that of the mounted man who did not see the sheriff halt, slide his Frontier Colt from its tied down holster, thumb back the hammer as he raised the revolver to aim it from the shoulder, sight aligned on Taggart.

But maybe the distraught rancher had heard the command and did as he was told. Or it could be he never intended to draw his gun unless he felt an undeniable compulsion. He continued to stare fixedly at the wagon as it rolled on to the square. Driven by Jethro, with Jack, Ryan and Coggins riding on the back. Then he snapped:

'Where's my daughter?'

His voice rang out clearly above the sound of the horses

and wagon as Jethro hauled on the reins, brought the rig to a halt. The pipe-smoking driver and the other three telegraph company men expressed surprise, which expanded into fear as they shifted their wide-eyed gazes: from Taggart with a hand on his holstered gun, to Fallows with his aimed revolver, and back again.

'What's that you want to know?' Jethro asked nervously as he took his pipe from between his near toothless gums.

'Kate! Where is she, damnit? I know you men know!'

'Taggart!' Fallows snarled. Began to advance at a measured pace, the Colt still held in a rock steady fist at arms length. 'If you don't——'

'Her and that kid that works with you!' the rancher roared on, totally ignoring the lawman. 'He's turned her head! She told me so! That boy, he ain't with you!'

Jack pushed off from the side of the wagon, frowned at Taggart as he said with slow deliberation: 'Davy Clavell ain't one for the drink, mister. Like me and the rest of my men. Reckon that's the reason he's not with us, maybe.

'Don't try to hand me that! I know what him and my girl are up to! I want to know where?'

He suddenly clasped his fist around the butt and drew his revolver. An ancient Remington that looked like it had hammered in a lot more nails than it had fired bullets.

Jethro grunted and threw himself sideways along the wagon seat. Jack cursed and pitched full length to the ground. Ryan and Coggins crouched low in the cover of the winch in the back of the wagon.

Just for a part second, Taggart expressed incredulous shock at this series of fast reactions. Then his rugged face showed fear as he looked down at the gun in his hand, next swung his head to peer at Fallows when the sheriff yelled:

'I warned you, you crazy bastard!'

Fallows seldom used bad language. Then, for the first time ever, he squeezed the trigger of his Colt to blast a bullet at a fellow citizen.

'Oh, my God, the sheriff's shot Arnie Taggart!' Ethan Brady rasped breathlessly. And his single eye peering from between the door and the frame expressed the same degree of shock as that seen on the face of the rancher, the lawman and most other witnesses to the unique event.

'That's how it looked from out here, too,' Adam Steele replied evenly as Taggart grunted, dropped his revolver, reached with the empty hand to clutch at the red stain starting to blossom across his upper left arm.

'But Len Fallows . . . He's not that kind,' the banker rasped.

Steele drawled softly: 'Reckon it was a case of being cruel to be kind.'

3

Steele looked hard at the shock-etched profile of Fallows' face, unsure if the lawman had intended to wound Taggart or to fire a warning shot but mis-aimed.

Then the abruptly wan-faced rancher dragged the hand away from his bullet-holed upper arm. Stared in horror at the blood on the palm and fingers. Raised his eyes to glare a pained rebuke at Fallows as he accused hoarsely: 'You shot me!'

'I didn't . . .' the lawman began, maybe starting to confirm Steele's guess it had been a mistake.

Probably only a handful of people closest to Fallows heard his opening words against the rising volume of shocked talk and the gasps and cries of women and children. Which gave the lawman time to scotch his initial intention. Compose himself, inject authority into his voice as he said, louder:

'I didn't want to shoot you, Taggart! I had to stop you doing something stupid you'd be sorry for later.'

There was a lessening of activity and noise as Jack picked himself up off the ground and Jethro, Ryan and Coggins got down off the wagon. Some people began to go about their interrupted business and most of the children started to head for home.

'One of you—Milly—and you, too, Rachel,' Lavinia Attwood commanded from between the wrought-iron gates of the schoolyard. 'I want you to go bring Doctor Mackay, please.'

Huey Attrill stirred up some mild ill temper as he forced a

way through the knot of men in the saloon doorway, eager to garner details of earlier events that had climaxed with the noon violence.

Jethro, pipe stem again clamped between his gums, the big bowl smokeless, began to lead the wagon team by the bridle of the nearside horse, headed for the front of the saloon. Jack, Ryan and Coggins trailed the rig and exchanged sour-toned complaints about almost getting killed by a crazy man for no good reason.

Fallows shoved his Colt back in the holster, strode toward the wounded man awkwardly hunched in the saddle. Reached him just ahead of Huey Attrill, as Taggart began to sway, looking paler and sicker by the moment.

Then Blanche Knight yelled: 'Thomas! Kindly ask those gentlemen there if they intend to frequent that filthy saloon or to have their lunch at my table today!'

The woman, who disapproved of strong drink, had been forced to come to terms with her misfortune in marrying a man who had developed into a heavy drinker. Because he was her husband, she sometimes needed to talk to Tom Knight. By referring to the telegraph company men like they could not hear, she more forcefully registered the degree of her disgust that they were obviously going to the saloon first rather than directly to her boarding house where they and Davy Cavell were bedding down in two rooms.

'Take some wine for your belly's sake, ain't that what the good Lord said in the Bible?' Jethro told her cheerfully before the narrow-chested, pot-bellied, swollen-nosed Knight could respond to his short, heavy wife.

His brother assured: 'We'll be there, soon as we've sharpened up our appetities for that fine cookin' you do, ma'am.'

Blanche countered: 'Thomas, tell them what's sharp is eatin' time! And that's twelve thirty! On the dot, you hear! Be there or they'll not get the chance to put their feet under my table again until suppertime!'

Taggart snarled a refusal of Fallows' offer to help to get down from his horse. But then he realised just how much strength had been drained by the shock of the gunshot on top of the burden of anxiety he carried for his missing daughter. He grudgingly accepted the assistance of Huey Attrill, a slightly built, angular-featured man who was not as old as he looked most of the time.

As many people were distracted by the raucously vocal ill-humour of Blanche Knight as continued to peer toward the trio of men in the centre of the square when she thundered, louder than ever:

'And you, Thomas! You get your useless self over here and lend a hand with settin' the table, you hear!'

Steele was about to start toward his horse as the rig halted and he acknowledged with a nod that Jethro and Jack had recognised him. But he paused when Lavinia Attwood signalled to him as she hurried out on to the square.

She halted beside the gunshot man, who still leaned on Attrill, as Fallows stooped to pick up the discarded revolver which he thrust under his belt. The anxiously frowning school-ma'am and the grimacing rancher exchanged brief words. Then their talk was curtailed by the sheriff, who snapped a curt command as he took up the reins of the horse: ignored Lavinia Attwood and Huey Attrill, ushered Taggart on ahead of him toward the office. Taggart made it on his own and Attrill started irritably toward his newspaper building.

'One good thing about what happened, Mr Steele,' Brady said as he swung the bank door wide again. Then changed the subject as Knight ambled disconsolately by, toward the boarding house, while other earlier customers and the four newcomers crowded into the saloon, calling to Harry Krim for drinks. 'How you doing, Tom?'

'I'm doin' lousy, Ethan, as you well know,' Knight complained bitterly. He glanced over his shoulder toward the Golden Gate and glimpsed the skinny, less than beautiful Joanne Morrison standing on the threshold of the stage line depot. Set the grimace more firmly on his liquor-dissipated face as he added, tone even more sour: 'Longer I stay married, the lousier I'm doin'. So you oughta bear that in mind, Ethan. If you're ever tempted to have Joe Marlow splice you to a female.'

Marlow was the parson at Providence's Protestant church

at the far south side of town. For some time it had been considered imminent Ethan Brady would ask the Widow Morrison to marry him.

The woman made a sound of deep disgust. Tom Knight went on home. And Brady struggled to recover his composure after he failed to think of a retort for Knight, or an apology for the woman. Then Joanne Morrison's son, who was dead set against his mother marrying anyone, called firmly to her to come inside, help him with some bookkeeping.

'If there's one trouble above all others with small-town living, Mr Steele, it's that everyone wants to have their noses in everyone else's business,' Brady growled. Mopped at his dry face with a handkerchief.

Steele reminded the banker: 'How's that the one good thing about what happened, feller?'

'Oh? What...? No, I was about to say... At least this time you didn't get yourself involved in the trouble.'

'And I am extremely pleased about that, also Mr Brady,' Lavinia Attwood announced as she completed crossing the square with her customary errect carriage. On her lightly powdered face was a concerned frown, which was displaced by a warm smile as she went on: 'I just wished to know how you have been keeping, Adam? It's been several days since you last visited town.'

'Just fine, Lavinia,' Steele replied as dropped his hand from tipping his hat. Displayed a matching smile to this woman who was as close as he had to a personal friend in the Providence River Valley where nobody else was more than an acquaintance. 'And you?'

She sighed and expressed mock glumness. 'I continue with the endeavour to retain my sanity while I attempt to instil some modicum of knowledge into the minds of the local fledglings. Most of who steadfastly decline to accept there is need to know anything of anything that comes out of a primer.'

She smiled again, invited: 'Join me for lunch, Adam? We have a few minutes to meet Blanche's dictated time?'

She was a permanent paying guest as the boarding house, and a mostly even-tempered personal friend of the volatile Blanche Knight.

'Grateful to you, but I reckon I'll get on back to Trail's End. Arlene fixed up a fine roast yesterday. Plenty left for tonight and I don't want to spoil my appetite for it.'

Brady, obviously unaware of the irony after his remark about the snoopiness of local citizens, had been waiting impatiently for an opening, now asked: 'Arnie Taggart make any mention of exactly why he's so all steamed up about his girl, Lavinia?'

She firmed her mouthline, but immediately revealed it was not the banker's inquisitiveness that irritated her. 'I know that Kate Taggart girl from teaching her until she left the school last summer. And I have little doubt Arnold Taggart has good reason to worry about her moral welfare. But if she is indulging in some sort of . . . If she does misbehave with the young man who works for the telegraph company—or any other young man—it will not be entirely his fault.'

'Brazen, uh?' Brady pressed eagerly.

Now Miss Attwood did glare at him, after she managed to hold herself back from giving an immediate confirmation of what he said: looked sheepishly at Steele, like she felt shame to be spreading gossip. But willing to do so on this far from usual occasion.

'She's just fifteen,' she hurried on. 'Apparently she told her father this morning she felt unwell and he sent her to bed while he went about his chores on their place. He cut his leg badly on some barbed wire and came back to the house to get a dressing. He saw Kate had left her bed, dressed and was gone. She had told him during an argument last evening that she was sweet on this young Clavell.'

'My, my,' Ethan Brady said, shaking his head.

Miss Attwood turned away, but paused for long enough to say: 'I'm glad to hear you are well, Adam. Perhaps we will eat together again on another occasion?'

He tipped his hat and she went on her way to the two story frame house with the 'Rooms for Rent' sign above the porch.

Then Brady, after an eager look at Steele, decided there was to be no more juicy gossip for the moment, withdrew into his bank.

At the hitching rail as he untied the gelding's reins, Steele heard the names of the gunshot rancher, his wanton young daughter and Davy Clavell drift out over the batwings on the aromatic tobacco smoke. He led his horse alongside the wagon and team, was about to swing up into the saddle, paused when hooves clopped and wheels turned on Main Street. Without undue haste. Moments later a familiar black and blue phaeton rolled out of the tree shade on to the brightly sun lit square.

Driving the rig was Thadius Mackay, a much overweight man who stood just over five feet tall. He had a florid face that displayed how unhealthy he was from overeating. But as a small-town doctor he was better than many Steele had come across during his drifting years. He knew his limitations, never attempted to exceed them.

'Somebody was shot, I was told by two very young ladies?' he called across the square to Steele, who was the only one still in the open.

'Law office, feller,' the Virginian supplied as he swung into the saddle.

Mackay halted his buggy. 'Oh, no, Len Fallows hasn't got himself hurt again?'

The lawman was almost fatally injured by a knife during a previous, more serious explosion of violence in Providence.

The door of the law office rattled open and Fallows, as willing to direct his ill-humour at the hapless medical man as anyone else, growled: 'No, it's not me, Thad! Come on over here. Patch up Arnie Taggart so we can go find his daughter for him.'

The injured rancher muttered something from the lock-up where, Steele knew from experience, there were three not so comfortable but adequate cots. Taggart's words were indistinct but the growling tone in which he spoke them was plain to discern.

Mackay set his buggy rolling again, steered it into a tight turn and reined in the horse out front of the law office. The rig tilted drastically to one side as he climbed out, toting his black leather bag of instruments and medicines. When he had stepped across the threshold, the door was closed firmly by Fallows: as if its slamming emphasised that the rest of the town was excluded from what was to take place within the granite building.

Steele heeled the gelding forward, reflecting on the truth Ethan Brady had spoken. It surely was a good thing on this occasion, when violence exploded less than a couple of hundred feet from where he stood, that he had been nothing more than a disinterested bystander. Fate had not conspired to involve him. And he had certainly not felt any kind of compulsion to take a hand.

The sense of contentment with which he had ridden so far through the timber from the ranch this morning now became re-established in Steele's mind as he angled his mount across the square toward the start of the north trail.

This time as he rode by he felt no instinctive urge to peer through the bars into the lock-up. Or through the glazed window of the law office out front of which stood Taggart's mount and Mackay's horse and buggy.

He reined in the gelding when the door of the meeting hall creaked open and he saw Arlene Forrester step out to shake a square of rag from which just a little dust flew. But the pretext served its purpose and the bulkily built black woman carried through the act by feigning surprise at unexpectedly seeing again one of her many employers.

'Happened to catch sight of you and Miss Attwood passin' the time of day, Mr Steele sir,' she was prepared to admit.

Steele tipped his hat. He was one of the few men in the Providence River Valley who extended any courtesy toward the negress who did such a large number of menial but necessary chores for so many people. 'Right, Arlene.'

'I figures she maybe asked you to eat with her at the Knight boardin' house? Like you done some times in the past?'

'Right, Arlene,' he told her again. Needed to work at keeping a smile off his face as he guessed what line the exchange was about to take.

'I'm real glad you didn't accept that offer to eat with the

schoolteacher, Mr Steele sir. And just you take care to heat that roast right through again tonight. And I'll see you first thing in the mornin', God willin'.'

Steele nodded. Allowed a quiet smile to turn up the corners of his mouth now, after the meeting hall door closed.

Blanche Knight was renowned as a cook and considered among the cleanest housekeepers in the valley. Only the black woman regarded herself a match for this combination. Thus, that her pot roast had won out against the prospect of whatever was for lunch at the boarding house was a triumph for Arlene Forrester.

Also, Steele knew, the negress was a little worried she could lose her job out at Trail's End: for she suspected the spinster schoolma'am was subtly setting her cap at the Virginian.

He ended the smile with a low grunt.

He liked good food sufficiently well to enjoy the fact that today he had been offered the choice of meals prepared by the two women who contested the reputation as finest cook in the valley. But as for Lavinia Attwood becoming more than a friend? Or any other woman...?

It was far from the first time he had found himself reflecting upon the notion that whatever else Trail's End had in its favour, the spread lacked female company.

He grunted again. More forcefully, the sound articulate in terms of how it conveyed irritability.

It was not the first time Arlene Forrester had obliquely triggered thoughts about the absence of a woman in his life: and always she implied this vacuum might be filled by Lavinia Attwood. But the schoolteacher was more firmly entrenched as a spinster than Steele had been a confirmed bachelor for so many years.

That deeply held belief had suffered a serious setback when he thought he had married a woman named Lucy Girard. There had been a handful of women before Lucy who, given the right set of circumstances, might well have become his wife. And, far more recently, a perhaps more likely marriage prospect than Lavinia Attwood had sought to become the missing element out at Trail's End. But, of course, Steele had never seen the tragically doomed Susan Lineker as such.

Hell, he told himself, if personal experiences provided insufficient reasons to persuade him marriage was not all that women—at the start—would have men believe, he had only to think back a few minutes. To Tom Knight's comments. And how the once married Arnie Taggart had been left with a daughter apparently set to cause him big trouble.

So, what the hell . . . ? He worked on a new smile, felt the expression lose its rigid falseness and mould easily on his face. It was like it had been earlier, almost. He had started to concern himself with problems that did not exist, unless he chose to create them. Should he ever feel troubled at not having female company out at the place, then was the time to reflect upon it as a problem.

Now, yet again, he held back on his intention to leave town when he heard a slow-moving rig rolling toward Providence. Like that driven by Jethro, this one came down the north trail.

Another flatbed, Steele saw. Drawn by a pair of sway-backed greys that showed signs of long travel. The offside team animal was slightly lame in the right hindleg and maybe this was why the driver maintained such an easy pace over the final hundred yards or so of trail to town.

He, and the man riding on the seat beside him, were both closer to fifty than forty. Both were skinny, unshaven and warmly attired in clothing that was the worse for wear. The driver was a head shorter than his six-feet-tall passenger. He had dark hair while the other man was ginger. Each wore a gunbelt slung around his waist outside the ragged and patched topcoat. Two rifle stocks jutted from between some crates on the sparsely laden wagon.

When the rig had first rolled into sight from around the curve in the timber-flanked trail, Steele thought the men were engaged in a low-toned, snarling argument. But when the tall passenger saw the Virginian sitting the saddle of a stationary horse in the gap between the two buildings flanking the end of the trail, he growled something to cut sharply across what the shorter man was saying. Then a fixed smile on his lean features before the driver had half turned to look toward Steele. And the driver was just two seconds late in fabricating his own smile to replace the former scowl.

He was first to briefly raise his battered hat, call a greeting. 'Good day to you, sir! Guess this must be . . .'

He allowed the query to hang unfinished for he had glimpsed the welcoming sign hung on the rear wall of the meeting hall. 'Yes, I see it is. And my business associate—Mr Cole Pope—and I, Albert Dean, sincerely trust we may indeed be welcome to the fine town of Providence.'

Steele wondered idly if Dean was always so effusive or if he was overly so in the wake of the sudden end to the heated disagreement with Pope.

There was sufficient space between the two buildings at the end of the trail for a horseman and a small wagon to pass. But Steele elected to wait for the newcomers to drive through on to the square. He had already nodded in acknowledgement when Dean named himself and Pope, now waited impassively until the driver hauled on his reins to halt the rig in the gap.

By then the smiles on the faces of both newcomers had lost every trace of falseness. Their deep set eyes even gleamed with something akin to excitement as they studied the sunlit expanse of the quiet town square at the middle of the day.

'Yes, indeed!' Dean chattered on. 'Cole and I would most certainly wish to be welcomed in such a fine-lookin' community.'

Steele said evenly: 'I reckon your nearside horse will welcome getting some attention from Harlan Grout, feller. And both animals some rest at his place.'

'This Harlan Grout is the local veternarian, Mr . . .?' Pope addressed Steele for the first time. He was much more slow-spoken. Like he was careful to choose each word before he voiced it.

'Liveryman, feller. But he can take care of minor horse ailments. Doc Mackay looks at the more serious ones.'

'A regular doctor practises here in Providence, too?' the still excited Dean hurried on. 'Mr . . .?'

'Steele, feller,' the Virginian replied. And saw the sudden sharp interest Dean showed in him for a moment. 'I reckon Providence has most of the services a small town needs.'

'Except for one, we understand,' Pope countered. 'Or so we were informed in the town of Broadwater back up the trail.'

Dean expanded: 'We hear that when somebody hereabouts is deceased, you folks need to send up to Broadwater for an undertaker?'

Steele did a double-take at the men, found he could, without calling upon much imagination, visualise them—suitably attired—interring the dead. He confirmed: 'Right.'

Dean spread a brand of smile across his unshaven, hollow-cheeked, sunken-eyed, pointed-jawed face that professional undertakers were inevitably able to summon and dismiss with apparent smooth ease. Then he said: 'Well, Cole and me are skilled carpenters, Mr Steele. And my Pa taught me his trade of carin' for the dear departed with sympathy for the bereaved.'

The exchange had obviously been overheard inside the meeting hall and the law office. Arlene Forrester made this apparent first, when she emerged from the meeting hall with her box of cleaning materials clutched tightly in fists held protectively high in front of her as she peered, wide-eyed with mistrust, at the two men on the wagon seat. Proclaimed vehemently:

'I wants you to promise me somethin', Mr Steele.'

'Arlene?' he asked, intrigued.

'If I dies——'

'Everyone dies, woman,' Pope put in.

'And them two is in the undertakin' business hereabouts, I wants you to have them people from up Broadwater take care of the arrangements for my earthly remains. I don't like the looks of——'

'My dear woman,' Dean cut in. 'Mr Cole Pope and I have travelled a whole lot of miles to reach here. We don't look our best, that's for sure. But if we set up business in this fine lookin' town, you can be sure we'll be——'

'Wants you to keep in mind what I said, Mr Steele sir,' the woman interrupted, more emphatic than before.

Then she started to waddle across the square, heading for a break in the trees to the west of the end of Main Street. Beyond which was a short cut to her shack some way south of where the Mission Farm Road bridge spanned the Providence River.

'Stupid——' Dean began to growl.

But Pope saw something in Steele's hard-set profile, as the Virginian looked after Arlene, that warned him it would be unwise to insult the negress within his hearing. And he broke in hurriedly: 'Well, there is one we have lost, Albert.' Then he modified the tone and pace of his voice. 'I think perhaps we should take the time to make ourselves more presentable before we announce our intention to other members of the local populace?'

He smiled at Steele, as if to invite an opinion on this view. But before the Virginian could speak, the law office door jerked open and Arnie Taggart stepped unsteadily outside.

His left arm was trapped across his chest in a sling knotted at the nape of his neck, and his sheepskin coat hung from his broad shoulders. His holster was still minus the elderly Remington. He looked as distraught as ever as he halted, turned his head to glare up at the strangers on the seat of the wagon and snarled:

'Diggin' a grave is damn dirty work! So before you clean yourselves up, that's the first thing you guys better do...!'

He moved, feet dragging in the dust, to his horse which had recovered from the earlier headlong gallop better than had the rancher from the gunshot. Continued:

'If you want to set yourselves up in the plantin' business around here...'

He halted beside his horse, swayed a little, took a deep breath: summoning the strength or maybe the courage to attempt to mount. Added grimly: 'If that's what you figure to do, it won't be so very long before you get your first carcase to bury.'

'You hold it right there, damnit!' Len Fallows roared as he strode from the law office, shrugging into a topcoat.

Pope said, his voice little more than a rasping whisper: 'As we understood it from the people we spoke to in Broadwater, Steele: lately there's been more fatalities from violence than by natural causes in this town?'

For a moment he looked about to dry-wash his hands in a

gesture of avariciousness: until his gaze was again caught by Steele's bleak glance.

Thadius Mackay squeezed out of the law office doorway in the wake of Fallows and began to urge Taggart to rest up for a while before he attempted anything strenuous. His advice cut across the voice of the lawman who made threatening demands the rancher should wait for him to get his horse out of the livery before he did anything about hunting for his daughter and Clavell.

Dean drew Steele's cold-eyed attention when he unwittingly began to explain just why he had directed such a pointed double-take at the Virginian when he revealed his name a few minutes ago. Said: 'I guess you have a hand of some kind in this business, uh?'

'How's that, feller?' the Virginian countered tonelessly.

Dean started to be perturbed, then shrugged and answered: 'The folks we talked with in Broadwater? They said Providence was a quiet little town until a man named Adam Steele came to live in the neighbourhood. Guess there ain't two guys named Adam Steele hereabouts?'

'Just the one,' Steele confirmed, took up the reins and made to heel his horse forward yet again.

Albert Dean was encouraged by the man's apparent easy acceptance of his reputation. As a total stranger he was unable to guess that under the thin veneer of nonchalance there could be latent ill-feeling on a dangerously short fuse. And he grinned companionably, lowered his voice to murmur as Steele rode close to him:

'More's the pity, uh? For men like Cole and me? The business we plan to start up here in Providence? If there were two guys like you . . .?'

Steele reined in his mount and turned to look the man full in his thin face across a distance of a couple of feet. And Dean caught his breath, abruptly provoked to a brand of fear on the brink of terror by the ice cold rage he could now see in the back of the jet black eyes of the Virginian.

Pope, who had already shown himself to be the more perceptive of the partners, started to excuse: 'I'm sure Albert didn't intend to——'

Steele became suddenly aware of what a fool he was to make an issue of this matter. Let himself be stirred up by a stranger who had no pre-knowledge to influence his judgment of the rumour he heard in a town ten miles away. A rumour, it had to be allowed, which had a sound basis in fact.

Although he was unable to drain all the shiny hardness out of his dark eyes, Steele did manage to shape his mouthline into a semblance of a gentle smile when he sighed. Murmured evenly:

'If people took as long to die as bad reputations, work for fellers in your line of business would be hard to come by.'

Dean breathed a deeper sigh than that vented by Steele. Growled with an insecure grin: 'Got you, mister.'

Steele heeled his horse forward and drawled wryly: 'Not for a while yet you don't.'

4

Steele had ridden just a short way out of town when he heard Albert Dean's voice again. Intoning in a patently fake sympathetic timbre to one or all three of the Providence men involved in the argument out front of the law office.

It was Taggart who cut in on the stranger with a snarled retort. Then Len Fallows started to add a harsh-toned comment. Which was interrupted by Cole Pope, speaking in his customary soft and measured manner: but apparently voicing the right kind of sense to capture the suddenly silent attention of his small audience.

Steele glanced over his shoulder then, came close to reining in his mount once again. But, as when he had been on the point of violently losing his temper with the hapless Albert Dean, he forced himself to check the initial urge to impulsive reaction.

It had been the firm conviction it was none of his business that caused him to deafen himself to the raised voices. So why the hell should he be interested in what the less excitably garrulous half of the Dean-Pope partnership was saying to draw the heat out of the situation?

So he did not halt the gelding. Kept fixedly facing front until he rounded that first curve of the north trail that carried him out of sight of town.

Moments later he heard a further tumult of several voices competing to make points. Then these faltered away or dropped to a level that failed to carry out into the timber.

Less than a minute later, as he rode past the last pole to be strung with telegraph wire before the men quit for the midday break, the aromatic fragrances of cooking food mingled with woodsmoke that was the final link with Providence was lost amid the stronger scents of evergreen pine and winter dampened turf and brush.

The scattered farmsteads and small ranches off to either side of the timbered valley were too distant for sight, sound or smell of their presence to carry down the spurs that connected them with the main trail.

Except for those infrequent occasions when business trips took him far from the Providence River Valley, Adam Steele had gotten out of the old habit of keeping a cautious watch on the surrounding terrain. When heading for or leaving town on this familiar stretch of trail he was usually totally at ease. As relaxed inside as would appear to a casual observer. Which was a mark of just how much he had changed from the kind of man certain people in Broadwater thought him to be.

But this early afternoon, he did not feel easy at all. He sensed heeltaps of the stillborn anger with Albert Dean continued to lay, sour and dank, someplace deep inside him. And the fact that he harboured such a sensation because of a brief conversation with a couple of strangers—about how he was viewed by another bunch of strangers ten miles away—concerned him: enough to make him jumpy.

He was not worried there could be danger lurking in the winter timber on all sides of him, of course. If that was to be—somebody from his past with a reason to carry a grudge was set to spring a deadly surprise on him, or a passing through road agent waited in ambush—then that was how the cards were going to fall. From a deck that had not been stacked.

Part of the good that came out of putting down roots at Trail's End was the way this new situation encouraged him to put such concerns to the back of his mind. Law-abiding horse ranchers who desired to stay clear of trouble did not spend too much time peering over their shoulders or pricking their ears for the first sound of lurking menace.

But today as he rode slowly toward the place he had made his home, he looked constantly around. Out of a sense of frustration: for he was burdened by futile anger at being angry.

Galloping the gelding might have helped relieve his feelings. Or he would have yelled a string of inarticulate curses at the trees. Blasted the Colt Hartford at the sky.

But such were the ways he had released his rages in the distant past: had helplessly surrendered to the dictates of the hot temper born in him.

During the War Between the States, and the violent peace which ensued, the avid desire to stay alive when surrounded by danger had served to help him control such impulses to crazily reckless reactions: forced him to keep his wits about him.

Now, Goddamnit, when he had no reason to fear a potential killer behind each tree or around every bend in a familiar road, he was burdened again with that need to control a mindless temper that could be ignited by the tiniest, often innocently struck, spark.

Abruptly, as he made to wrench his gaze from one side of the trail toward the other, something he saw made him check the move. And he hauled unnecessarily hard on the reins to pull up the gelding. While his facial muscles took just a part of a second to alter the scowl caused by self anger into a grimace of horror.

His horse snorted and quivered beneath him. He neither knew nor cared whether the gelding sensed the presence of death, or simply registered disapproval of the way Steele had so abruptly halted the easy walk.

He looked more carefully about him: and unlike moments ago when he was seeking an outlet for his emotions in any kind of physical action, he now saw in precise detail what he looked at.

Recognised he was something over half way between town and the point where the river and the trail came close, where Timber Creek and the spur up to Trail's End angled off to the west. Maybe a couple of hundred yards past the place where he had first met with the telegraph company workers on his way into Providence.

The dead girl lay beside a thicket of leafless brush a hundred feet off the trail to the east. Clearly visible only if a passerby on the trail happened to peer in that direction: because he was searching for her, or he needed to look any place but inside himself to get rid of a futile anger he had no wish to indulge?

Steele grunted irritably as he swung out of the saddle: acknowledged the faulty logic of the conclusion. And what the hell did it matter, anyway? Then he felt his grimace alter to impassiveness as he realised he had jumped to another conclusion: because he had linked what he saw from a distance with what he knew of preceding events, not all of them related.

Kate Taggart—for that was surely who it was, slumped on her side, back toward the trail—was not necessarily dead. Just because his abused horse reacted the way he did. And there were a couple of undertakers in the area. And Arnie Taggart had threatened to kill the kid who might or might not have hurt his daughter.

He rasped a curse through gritted teeth. Thudded a tight fist into an open palm. Wrenched the Colt Hartford from the boot. And immediately—after he wrapped a hand around the frame, curled a thumb over the hammer and clenched the other hand around the barrel of the rifle—felt icily calm.

Still angry at many things and his responses to them: but with the emotion totally under control, compressed into a small cold ball at the pit of his belly now. He could think clearly. He was not looking for trouble, but if it came his way he was ready to meet it. And deal with it: old style.

Then, about to swing away from his calmed mount, he paused. Listened. Grimaced again, fleetingly, when he heard hooves slowly clopping toward him. From the direction of town. Two horses, not hauling a wagon. He guessed they were carrying Taggart and Fallows and a moment after he made this assumption he felt the cold anger melt out of him.

Alive or dead, the female form slumped on the grass in the timber—whether or not it was the missing fifteen year old—had nothing to do with him. He had just happened to be in town when it was widely learned Kate Taggart had gone missing. Just happened to pass by here and catch sight of——

'Steele!' There was tension in Len Fallows' yell.

'What's wrong there?' Taggart demanded to know, in a tone tremulous with anxiety.

Before the Virginian had time to answer, the rancher seemed to sense something of the dreadful truth; thudded in his heels, galloped his horse toward Steele. Fallows was quick to command speed from his mount. Then, as Taggart hauled one handed on his reins to bring his horse to a skidding, snorting halt that came close to unseating the disabled rancher, the lawman brought his animal to an easier stop.

Fallows drew the Frontier Colt clear of his holster as he swung to the ground, demanded grimly: 'What's the rifle for, Steele?'

Taggart started to climb gingerly down from his jittery horse, his head swinging from side to side as his anguished eyes sought to spot for themselves the reason why Steele had taken the rifle from the boot.

And while the lawman still peered quizzically at the Virginian with the Colt Hartford canted across the front of his body, the rancher saw the slumped form in the timber.

Perhaps he had his wits about him sufficiently to recognise the drab grey dress, the dull blonde hair. Or maybe he was too stunned by shock to see anything so specific. Whatever, he uttered a strangled cry that could have been a despairing voicing of his daughter's name. This as he half fell to the ground now: would have crumpled to the trail had not Fallows whirled toward him, thrust out an arm to steady the tormented man.

As he did this, the sheriff found his attention captured by the sight upon which Taggart's shocked gaze was fixed and he rasped: 'Oh, dear God, no!'

Thus Steele had no need to respond to his query.

Taggart tore free of the supporting grip and staggered off the trail into the timber at an ungainly run. Heading along a natural pathway through the trees toward the small clearing in which the girl lay.

Fallows hurried after him.

'It's her! That bastard! The bastard kid had his way with

my Kate! And killed her! Kate! Kate!'

Exertion and dread made Len Fallows sound as breathless as Taggart when he yelled: 'Take it easy! We don't know a damn thing for sure until——'

'Shut up, shut up, damnit!' the rancher roared as he slithered to a halt, dropped to his knees beside the slumped form. Reached out with his free hand to cup the girls's face. Then began to murmur softly as his big body became wracked with silent, shuddering sobs.

Fallows stood over the grief-stricken man kneeling beside the unfeeling girl. Pushed the revolver back in his holster after he had stiffened in response to the enraged demands for silence yelled at him.

Behind the lawman, Steele took a one-handed grip on the rifle, sloped it to his shoulder, finger withdrawn from the trigger, thumb off the hammer. He glanced occasionally from side to side, back over his shoulder. Not looking for a threat to himself, as when he had foolishly over-reacted a few moments ago. But if Davy Clavell was anywhere nearby and showed himself, it was plain the youngster would need protection from the grieving rancher.

Which, the Virginian told himself with a silent sigh, was down to Sheriff Len Fallows. Hell, he had just gotten through with deciding that none of this was anything to do with him!

Suddenly Arnie Taggart became immobile and utterly silent. For maybe two stretched seconds he stared down at the girl. Next up at the man standing over him, and rasped:

'She's alive! My Kate ain't dead, damnit! She's breathin'!'

Fallows made to step around the father and daughter. But Taggart sprang to his feet. Turned his back on the girl and flung his sound arm to the side in a gesture that barred the sheriff and the Virginian from getting to her.

'Why?' Fallows asked tautly.

'No, not yet!' The rancher wriggled his body so the sheepskin coat slid off his shoulders to the ground. 'My girl ain't decent to be seen. That sonofabitch ripped open her clothes to have his way with her! Hold back now, or I'll——'

'Sure,' Fallows conceded. 'But don't waste too much time, Taggart. Quicker we get her to Doc Mackay the better.'

With some reluctance because of his concern for the young girl, he followed Steele's example; turned his back on father and daughter. Then they heard Taggart's laborious breathing while he hurried to wrap the limp form in the coat, hampered by one arm in a sling.

Then Fallows muttered: 'It looked like you just that second spotted her when we came around the bend in the trail, Steele?'

'Right, Sheriff.'

'You didn't see anything else?'

'No.'

'Nobody else?'

'No.'

The lawman left a pause that was layered with suspicion, then probed: 'You had that fancy rifle of yours out of the boot.'

'Before I heard you coming, Sheriff,' Steele told him, evenly. 'Had first sight of the girl here while my mind was somewhere else. It just happened I felt the need to take out the rifle.'

Taggart still made sounds of struggling with covering his daughter's partially unclothed form. Along with some groans, almost sobs, of frustration that he could not do so quickly with one disabled arm.

Steele sensed Len Fallows' eyes fixed upon his impassive profile: guessed the lawman was intrigued to discover a side of him which he had not realised existed. Then the Providence sheriff sighed, rasped softly:

'Yeah, same way I just happened to shoot the poor guy back in town.'

There was another lull in the talk, filled with nothing between Steele and Fallows except for sounds made by Taggart. Then, at length, the rancher announced:

'Okay, now I need some help with her.'

The others turned to see he had done a more than adequate job of covering the girl's exposed body from their eyes. For Kate Taggart was just a couple of inches over five feet tall and so her father's coat almost enveloped her: just her ankles and feet showed at the bottom and her head at the top. He had buttoned the coat from the hem to neck, overlapped the large lapels.

Steele allowed he had probably glimpsed the girl a number of times in town, but he had no ready memory of the face he could see clearly now she was lying on her back. He had seen from the start she was as slender as most girls of her age. Her face had that kind of immature prettiness, with a basic bone structure and a perfect complexion to suggest she could turn into something of a beauty in later years.

Which, he recalled, was much the same opinion he had formed of Davy Clavell. Kate Taggart's blonde hair, straight and cut short, was almost the same shade as that of the boy.

'That stranger sure enough was right, uh?' Taggart said hoarsely as he continued to squat on his haunches on the far side of the girl whose childish prettiness was at present marred by a large yellow and black swelling on her right temple. Then he cleared his throat to ask: 'One of you men gonna lift her and carry her to my horse?'

'I'll take care of that, Mr Taggart,' Fallows offered quickly, perhaps using the courtesy title in deference to the anguish the rancher now had good reason to feel. A much subdued degree of the emotion now, like the finding of the girl, unconscious and sexually assaulted, but at least alive, had drained the man of the will to generate the kind of burning rage he had felt before.

Fallows stooped, inserted both arms under the coat-wrapped form. Taggart made to rasp something, maybe a demand for the lawman to take care. But instead he clamped his lips tightly together as he used his free hand to steady his daughter in the rock-firm grip of Fallows as the tall lawman unfolded to his full height with concentrated care.

'You all right with her, Sheriff?' Steele asked.

'Sure, I'm fine.' He sounded surprised. 'There's hardly anything of her. But then she is just a kid.'

'Won't be any damn thing of another kid except for dead weight when I——' Taggart began to snarl grimly as he went after the lawman, back along the narrow track through the trees toward the horses on the trail.

'Take it easy, Mr Taggart,' Fallows advised again. 'Time

enough for considering what we do next when Kate's getting the best care Doc Mackay can give her.'

Taggart grunted his intention to argue the point. But after he looked over Fallows' shoulder into the wan, bruised face of the girl, her head rested on the sheriff's upper arm he bit back on the words. Then, needing to occupy his mind with talk, he turned to look at Steele who brought up the rear.

'Those two strangers on the wagon you were yakkin' with in town, mister?'

Steele nodded. 'Pope and Dean.'

Taggart faced front again. 'Didn't get their names. The tall one, he told us how him and his partner saw my little girl and the Clavell kid foolin' around at some kinda game out here.'

Fallows reminded tensely: 'They didn't name Clavell, Mr Taggart.'

The rancher spat to the side, countered scornfully: 'How many blond haired kids are there runnin' around in this valley that my Kate's likely to . . . And after she'd told me herself she was sweet on that one?'

'Okay,' Fallows allowed wearily. 'We'll find the boy and hear what he has to say. Unless Kate regains consciousness first and tells us it was another——'

As they emerged from the timber on to the trail, the rancher interrupted, his rage rising again: 'Kate'll likely make up some kinda story! The way she's so struck with that kid!'

'Yeah. Okay. All right. Let's leave it awhile.' The lawman's tone of voice and the glittering light in his dark eyes showed he was close to losing his temper with the pigheaded attitude of the man who had wantonly squandered the sympathy he deserved. 'Now: how d'you want us to get your daughter to town? Or maybe you want to stay here with her while I ride on in and bring Thadius Mackay out here with a wagon for Kate to ride on?'

Now, for long moments, Arnie Taggart was lost for words, his mind vacant of thoughts. His rugged face showed many fleeting expressions of pathetic confusion as he was presented with making a decision outside of finding and punishing Davy Clavell. He looked from Len Fallows who stood unmoving with the shallowly breathing girl in his arms, to

Steele who was at his horse, sliding the Colt Hartford back in the boot. Then he blurted:

'What...? I guess... Look, I figured to ride with Kate on my horse. But with this damn arm the way it is——'

'A quarter mile is all it can be to Providence,' Fallows cut in on the confused man, who was acting with indecision. 'I can walk with her that far like this. You take care of the horses?'

The rancher was eager to do as the lawman suggested. And now somebody else had made the decision, he was able still to suppress his ill-feeling toward the boy he held responsible for his daughter's suffering. Willing to fall in with whatever was suggested until Kate was getting medical attention. He nodded vigorously, took up the reins of his own and Fallows' mounts.

The Virginian swung astride his gelding, made no move to wheel the horse in the direction of town, so showed he did not intend to ride in with the other two men.

Taggart was unconcerned at this and it almost seemed he had forgotten Steele was there. Fallows eyed the Virginian bleakly for a few moments, then said:

'It appears you want no more part in this, Steele?'

'Way I see it, it's none of my business, Sheriff.'

Fallows looked like he might reluctantly let the matter rest there. But then halted his move to turn away from Steele, asked: 'If I need to get a posse together, I can't count on your help?'

This acted to trigger Arnie Taggart out of his mood of pre-occupation. Before Steele could respond to the lawman, the rancher snapped:

'So to hell with him, Sheriff!' He shared an almost murderous glare equally between the man disinclined to help and the other who had a duty to find and protect the man responsible for the attack on Kate Taggart. 'I don't figure there'll be any trouble gettin' volunteers to hunt down the sonofabitch that——'

'Sure, Mr Taggart,' Fallows cut in. And now sounded too weary to bear his slightly-built burden for more than a few paces. But it was just his spirit that was temporarily drained. His tall, lean frame remained as strong as ever as he moved alongside the man with the horses. As they started along the trail, he glanced over his shoulder to growl the rebuke: 'You sure have changed, Steele.'

The Virginian nodded, replied flatly: 'If I haven't, feller, I sure have wasted a lot of time trying.'

'If it should just happen you run across anything that has a bearing on this business, you'll do the right and proper thing?'

'What I'll do is my best, Sheriff.'

'Somethin' you can do for me if you run into the Clavell kid, Steele?' Taggart said grimly. 'You tell him from me——'

'Sure,' Steele interrupted. 'I reckon I've got your message for the telegraph boy.'

5

Steele rode northward at a pace just a little faster than the two men headed south. Allowed himself an unrestricted mind so that his conscience was free to torment him with guilt if that was the way it was to be.

But while he remained aware of the sounds of men and horses moving away behind him, and for as long as it took him to get to the spur in the trail, angle off to the west, splash across the ford and start to ride uphill alongside Timber Creek, he felt easy in his mind.

Even a little self-satisfied with how he had handled the situation as a law-abiding rancher: who just happened through a series of accidents to have gotten himself slightly involved on the fringes of the troubles of another law-abiding rancher.

He had done all that was necessary in the circumstances, he considered. After that initial impulse to do what he would have regarded as necessary in the drifting days of the past. Then, fortunately, Taggart and Fallows showed up: one man required by family ties and the other by his job to take positive hands in the business.

Steele rode up the fir-clad slope, still feeling good. Then across the plateau where the pine trees became mingled with mixed timber which at this time of year cast less shade from the bright but cold sun. And when he reached the square arch of timber with the legend 'Trail's End' scorched into the plank above the gate, he suddenly felt a cold shiver run through him. Knew this tremor had nothing to do with the temperature which had not got any colder since midday.

He swung to the ground, unfastened the gate, opened it, led his horse through and reclosed and fastened it. Then cursed; an outlet for tension he had seldom allowed himself as a drifting saddletramp who often found himself profiting from other people's misfortunes. But he was using oaths more and more lately, it seemed.

He got back in the saddle, started over the final leg of the journey home. In fact, rode on land that was as much a part of his home as the house.

His conscience began to prick.

He was a rancher himself now, damnit. The same as Arnie Taggart. Both of them parts of the same community. And surely being a part of a community meant helping others who had troubles within that community. At least offer to lend a hand?

Now, as he emerged from the largely leafless winter timber, rode along the final five hundred feet of track between the near empty crop fields south of the house, the yard and the corral, Adam Steele was in a far less congenial frame of mind than when he had set out from there something over a couple of hours ago.

And not for the first time he began to have bitter thoughts about the compromise he had made when he decided to take on Trail's End. To build it with hour after hour of day-in, day-out hard labour into something he so ardently desired.

But even at the outset he had acknowledged it could never be exactly that: because the town of Providence was nearer than a mile as the crow flew. And, too, there were the other working ranches and farms scattered along the sides of the river valley.

Damn people!

How could any man like having people around him? How could anyone subscribe to the theory that a trouble shared was a trouble halved? In his book, sharing trouble simply meant that more people than necessary were screwed up by a problem not of their making.

Then, as he reined in his gelding on the centre of the yard, allowed his gaze to rake the scene on all sides of him, he started to feel the sourness of this mood drain out of him. What was done, was over. In a major respect was like the future. Not worth worrying about unless it brought repercussions.

Now he surveyed the land with a sense of achievement at how good the place looked after all that hard work had been put in on it. But, like always on his return to Trail's End, he looked also for signs of anything wrong.

Checked that nature had not conspired to upset his plans, or malicious intruders had not been by to disrupt the smooth progress of turning this piece of country into the best little horse ranch in the state of California. Maybe even the best to be found west of the Mississippi: or, when his horizons were restricted by sound common sense, as good as he ever wanted it to get.

Today, everything appeared fine in the clear winter sunshine.

The house, with an occasional trace of dark smoke wisping from the chimney, and the barn seemed to be exactly as he had left them. The chestnut mare and her six-week-old foal in the corral looked healthy, both of them happy to be alive after the gruelling delivery. Far out on the other side of a four-hundred yard wide expanse of pasture beyond the corral, two more mares and the stallion cropped contentedly close to the base of Rocktop Hill.

While from out back of the barn came the sound of the hog rooting in his pen, the clucking of the chickens he had confined to their run before he left town. He failed to spot the milk cow, but this probably meant only that the Fresian was grazing close to the sink hole or on the bank of the creek out behind the barn.

The hog, the fowl and the cow were replacements for the animals wantonly slaughtered while he was away on a horse-buying trip. By the same people who killed Billy Baxter...

But that was all in the past.

He dismounted: led the gelding toward the timber barn. The doors were open, just as he had left them, so morning air could circulate freely through the building, help to kill the pungent odour of the creosote he had painted on the underside of the roof yesterday.

He felt totally at peace with the world again: and with

himself. Disassociated from everyone and everyone else's troubles. Satisfied that, whatever his own problems, he would take care of them in due course. Without need of help.

He stooped to unbuckle the cinch beneath the belly of the gelding. Froze when he heard somebody suck in a deep breath. Readied himself to whiplash erect, reach for the Colt Hartford: or the knife. Whichever offered the best chance to counter an attack by whoever waited for him in the barn.

'Mr Steele?'

Apprehension close to dread gave the voice a far more youthful timbre than he recalled. To the extent he would not have recognised it from this tense calling of his name did he not know Davy Clavell had good reason to be deeply afraid.

He remained in the stoop. His head raised high enough so he was able to peer into the sun-shadowed, creosote-smelling barn. Where he saw the youngster standing just beyond the threshold, hat crushed between both his constantly moving hands, the look on his immaturely handsome face suggesting he was on the verge of breaking into tears.

'Mr Steele, there's been some real bad trouble.'

The Virginian nodded, grunted, unfastened the cinch.

The boy stepped forward, pleaded tremulously: 'Mr Steele, I don't know what to do?'

The man straightened up, answered evenly: 'How about let's start a club, kid?'

6

The Virginian was gripped by an almost overwhelming desire to lunge into the barn, smash a fist into the youngster's finely-chiselled face.

Immediately, this impulse was followed by another: to yell at Clavell at the top of his voice. Give impetuous free rein to his rage as he roared at him to get the hell away from him. Out of his barn and off his place. Grow up, take care of his own lousy troubles.

This within the space of a few stretched seconds. While Davy Clavell watched him levelly with his wide, clear blue eyes dominating an expression that suggested he would comply instantly with whatever the Virginian demanded of him. Go to Providence and turn himself over to the sheriff, maybe. Or even make himself available for whatever brand of punishment Arnie Taggart had in mind for him.

Then the youngster swallowed hard, and muttered despairingly: 'You know?'

By now Steele's initial reactions had run their gamut without breaking the surface. And he felt as calm inside as he obviously looked to the boy who was no longer on the brink of tears.

Clavell had become a lot less terrified than he was a few seconds before. Like he now felt confident he was going to get help from Steele.

'Yeah, I know you're in trouble.'

'I didn't do it, Mr Steele. I didn't kill Kate Taggart.'

'I know that, too.'

Clavell was suddenly incredulous. Then he started a smile that immediately went out of control: became a shrill laugh of deflating tension. He blurted between guffaws: 'Thank God. So they've found the one who——'

'All they've found is the girl, kid. Not dead though. Unconscious right now. You want to finish unsaddling my horse? Then turn him loose in the corral?'

'What?' the abrupt switch of mood from the depth of despair to near hysterical relief had almost drained him of physical strength. He swayed, staggered a few steps but had the presence of mind to steer himself to the side, where he could reach out for the support of the doorframe.

'And after you've done that, like you to step on over to the house.'

Steele did not wait for any kind of acknowledgement before he slid the Colt Hartford out of the boot, turned and angled across the yard. Pushed open the unlocked front door mid-way between the two windows, entered the one-room timber and fieldstone house.

He needed to make a deliberate effort to void his mind of all thought this time, as he first leaned the rifle against the wall just inside the doorway. Then he stirred the ashes in the stove to uncover some red embers, tossed on some more fuel. Put coffee in the pot and the pot on the stove. Next moved away from the kitchen area of the room to the half which was both parlour and bedroom. Where, piled on the easy chair between the window and a home made bookcase, were the workclothes he had taken off last night.

He had gotten out of the suit and had on work pants and shirt when knuckles tentatively hit on the door.

'Come on in, kid,' he called as he dropped into the chair and pulled on his boots. Gestured that Clavell should go to the far end of the room. 'You can see where the mugs are on that shelf. Soon as the coffee's ready, you pour. I hardly ever eat this time. Today I'm sure not eating until supper.'

'Last thing I am is hungry, Mr Steele.'

The Virginian rose from the chair, hung the thuggee scarf around his neck, kerchief fashion, began to button his shirt. Asked:

'You want to take a seat at the table now, tell me what happened?'

Clavell closed the door, almost reverently like he was entering a church, went to the table and sat down. Chewed on the inside of his left cheek for a while, then asked: 'Kate's in pretty bad shape, uh?'

He dug the makings out of a shirt pocket, but his hands began to shake badly and he replaced the tobacco poke without even attempting to roll a cigarette.

'I don't know,' Steele answered as he came to the table, tucked his shirt tails into his pants. 'But for a kid who was raped and knocked out she could be worse, I guess. The sheriff and her father took her to town to Doc Mackay.'

'Oh, God!' He set his elbows firmly on the table, cupped his hands and pushed his face into them. Not just the hands shook now.

'Bawling won't help anything, kid,' Steele told him.

Clavell gave a final shudder, jerked up his head and shook it, a defiant expression on his dry-eyed face. 'I ain't cryin', Mr Steele.' He swallowed hard. 'You got any idea how long Kate's liable to stay unconscious?'

'No.'

'Maybe she could even die, you think?'

'I wouldn't know.'

'God, if she don't come out of it . . . Tell what happened to her . . . They'll be comin' after me, won't they?'

'The sheriff spoke of forming a posse to hunt you down, kid.'

Clavell squeezed his eyes tight closed, gulped.

Steele told him: 'If the girl doesn't come out of it and get you off the hook, it'll be Sheriff Fallows' duty to find you, hold you out of harm's way until you stand trial.'

'But I don't have a chance to . . . Out of harm's way?'

'If she comes out of it and says it wasn't you who did that to her, her father won't believe her. He'll come looking for you anyway. A trial isn't what he has in mind.'

'Oh, God.'

'Reckon it's best you should know just what kind of a spot you're in, kid. No sense in painting you a pretty picture that's not a true one. Now, you want to tell me how things happened from your side?'

'Then what?'

'Like I said at the start, I don't know, kid. You came here to hide out for some reason, and——'

'I just took off without no idea of which way I was goin' after I found Kate like that!' he hurried to defend his actions. 'I didn't have no idea! All I wanted was to get away from——'

'Whatever the reason, you're here,' Steele broke in. 'I have to figure out what I'm going to do about that. And unless you sell me on your version of what happened to the girl, my inclination's to turn you over to the sheriff in——'

'Please, I——'

'That's the third idea that occurred to me. First I was going to beat hell out of you for bringing trouble here. Next I was going to kick your butt off my place. Matter of fact, I still haven't made up my mind to abandon either of those ideas.'

Davy Clavell was quick to start his explanation. 'Me and Katy, we been sparkin' since I come here to Providence on Jack O'Mally's work gang, Mr Steele. I met up with her the first day. Jack and Jethro, Kenny Coggins and Pete Ryan, them guys spend most of their spare time in the saloon. I ain't much of a drinker. Me and Katy, we... Well, we pitched a little woo, so to speak.'

'In the dark.'

'Uh? No, not always. We sometimes——'

Steele shrugged. 'I never keep up much with town gossip. Do happen to know, though—on account of he told me—the girl's Pa never knew about his daughter and you until she told him about it last night.'

The boy looked shamefaced. 'Well, yeah. We weren't doin' nothin' wrong. But we did as much as we could to keep it quiet we was seein' each other. Whenever she could get away from her old man and I weren't workin' on the telegraph. That was Katy's idea to keep it quiet, Mr Steele.'

The coffee pot boiled over noisily and the angry hissing of steam distracted Clavell. He stared at the stove, surprised, then at the Virginian.

'I started it off,' Steele reminded. 'Asked you to——'

The boy rose irritably from the table, went to do as he had been bid. Preoccupied, he made to pick up the pot with a bare hand, so burned himself. He cursed and shared parts of an angry glare between the pot and Steele when he realised the Virginian could have warned him but had remained silent. Then, as he used a cloth, he calmed down: and continued with his account as he brought mugs and the pot to the table, poured each of them a coffee.

'She kept tellin' me what a real strict old man she had. That if he found out about us he'd make sure Kate never got away from their ranch to come see me. And maybe he'd beat up on me as well. The only ones that knew about us, far as I could tell, were the guys in the work gang. But they're a pretty good bunch. Pete Ryan, he can make trouble if he's a mind to. But he didn't for us. They all of them ribbed me a lot, but I could take that okay.'

'Let's get to this morning, Steele prodded as he hooked a gloved hand around the brimful mug of coffee Clavell pushed across the table to him.

'Yeah, I——' He sucked in a deep breath, let it escape as a long sigh. Clasped both hands around his mug as if to warm them. Was doubtless pleasantly aware of the heat on his palms, but knew it would take much more than hot coffee to reach deep down and bring comfort where he really needed it. Then he went on:

'We'd fixed it that we'd see each other tonight. If she could get away from her old man. Nothin' was ever certain. It always depended on her makin' up stories and her old man believin' them. Well, she showed up this mornin' instead. Out where I was workin'. Not so long after you come by. Jack said I could take some time to be with her and we went off on our own. It was pretty close to the quittin' hour for the mornin' work anyway.'

Steele sipped the coffee, found his gaze often wandered to the window at the parlour-bedroom end of the house. From where he sat at the pine table, this offered a view out over parts of the crop fields and the track between them: not quite to where the spur emerged from the timber. If anyone came to Trail's End, this was invariably the way they approached: if their visit was not a surreptitious one.

He was beginning to get a bad feeling about how things were developing. Started to regret he did not send Clavell packing as soon as the kid revealed his presence in the barn. Or did not make him a prisoner, take him into town. Now, the way things were shaping up, he could well find himself on the side of a stranger, opposed to the community of which he was a part, like it or not.

'What's wrong?' Clavell was abruptly anxious. He had seen some of the many glances Steele directed out of the window.

'Not a thing either of us can do anything about right now, I reckon. What happened this morning?'

Clavell needed a few moments to collect his thoughts, pick up the thread of the tale from where he had left off before he was unsettled by doubt. Then he remembered, nodded, and continued:

'She told me right off we were in bad trouble, Mr Steele. Her old man had guessed somethin' was up, how she was always makin' excuses to leave their place lately. And she blurted the truth to him: last night, like he told you. They had a blazin' row about it.'

'This mornin' she made out she was sick. And when he went off to do the ranch chores, she sneaked away. She said she wanted me to take her away from Providence. She wouldn't go back to her Pa, no matter what. I was real scared, told her she had to. Said we'd go together. But she reckoned her old man would tear me limb from limb.

'Then she ran off. And I went after her. She kept callin' out to me. Then started to laugh some. She could . . . She can be real crazy like that sometimes. It was like we were playin' some kinda stupid kid's game of hide and seek. Then it all went quiet.'

It was now exceptionally quiet outside the house, too. Or maybe it had been so all along, Steele allowed. No sounds of the stock or of birds in the timber, nor the rippling of the slow-running creek able to reach in with both the front and rear doors firmly closed. It certainly was the first time it had been this silent within the house. Only the flames of the fire in the stove made tiny crackling sounds as Davy Clavell privately recalled his terror in the timber and Steele waited for the boy to reach the conclusion of his story.

Then Clavell suddenly rose from the table. Spun on his heels. Went to the window immediately behind where he had been seated. Peered out, his face pressed close to the glass. Then he whirled to glare at Steele with something close to hatred in his clear blue eyes. Next moved a hand to reach for the revolver in his holster. But he was able to check the impulse to draw the gun. Though anger proved less easy to control as he accused in strangled tones:

'You know somethin' you ain't told me! They're comin' here, ain't they?'

Steele said evenly: 'Clavell, take it easy.'

'You keep lookin' through the window!' he shot another frightened glanced out at the sun bright afternoon. 'The sheriff's posse is comin' so you can join it, is that it? Or I left tracks gettin' here? You've come to make me confess to what I never done and then ...'

He vented a despairing gasp.

'No, you're wrong, kid.'

'I don't believe that!'

Steele sighed, shrugged, raised the mug in a two-handed grip to sip more coffee. Held it firmly in front of his lower face as his voice hardened. He spoke over the rim, through the steam that rose off the coffee.

'So take off. If you do that, though, and I get asked, I'll have to tell them you were by.'

'I'll want one of your horses!'

The desperate decision made, his temper was under control. There was not a trace of impetuosity in his youthful face as he brought his right hand down, fisted it around the butt of the holstered revolver. It was a Frontier Colt and, like the weapon of Arnie Taggart, it was a working man's handgun. Had seen more service as a hammer than the purpose for which it was manufactured.

The Virginian, in even firmer control of himself than the youngster, lunged into a much faster series of moves than he did. Came erect, both hands thrust forward. Tilted the mug. Hurled its contents across the width of the table and four more feet: full into the face of the startled boy.

The coffee was some way off being boiling hot by now. But its heat plus the shock of the fluid splashing against his flesh triggered a scream from Clavell as he brought up both hands to his head, clawed to clutch his face.

Fully upright, his chair fallen backwards with the impetus of his move, Steele stepped around the table. Was directly in front of the kid as Clavell realised he had not been scalded, dragged his hands down from his dripping features. Was suddenly frozen in terror as he saw the intensity of feeling so starkly visible at such close quarters in the face of Adam Steele.

This as the Virginian reached out his left hand, grasped the boy's coat lapels, twisted the fabric. At the same time drew back his right hand clenched into a fist, poised to smash it into the terror-stricken face.

Steele could feel the rigidity of his own face, knew it had become set into a grimace that maybe was close to expressing the full degree of his anger toward the boy he had at his mercy.

'Please... I'm sorry... I didn't...'

Steele experienced a tightness across his chest. It quickly reached painful proportions, and for one awesome moment he thought he had been driven to the point of a heart seizure by the enormity of his resentment against this terrified kid. But then he heard the whistling sound through his gritted teeth: realised he had been involuntarily holding his breath. And with the noisy venting of stale air out of his lungs, he felt all of the tension, some of his anger with Clavell, drain from him.

'Honest, I didn't——'

'Shut your damn mouth,' Steele commanded tonelessly, trapped the boy's blue eyes with the icy stare of his black ones. 'Just don't say one word until I tell you.'

Clavell swallowed hard, felt the need to acknowledge what he had been told: managed a nod of sorts within the restriction set by the way Steele's fist, clutching his lapels, was pushed up almost to touch his jaw. The kid's hands remained hanging limply at his sides.

Steele took two carefully controlled breaths. In a quiet, evenly pitched tone that would have been totally lacking in menace had not he shown such an intense expression, held the boy as he did, with his free hand clenched into a fist ready to crash into his jaw, he said:

'You best take care over all you say and do from now until the time your number comes up, kid. Whether Taggart kills you today. Or you hang by due process. Or you die in bed at ninety-five from weariness with living. Because every second you got left to you is borrowed time. So you be grateful to be alive. Right now, you be grateful I'm not the man I used to be.'

He released his hold on the coat lapels, dropped both arms to his sides. Backed off from the still rigid youngster, wide-eyed and gulping with fear. He knew there was no pretence in Clavell's attitude right then. But he did not trust the present fear to stay constantly dominant over suspicion of a double-cross. So he directed many glances toward the kid as he stooped to pick up his mug from where he had dropped it to the floor. Then replaced the coffee pot on the stove to re-heat and gave Clavell his full attention when he reminded:

'Then it went quiet?'

'What?' It was little more than a croak, barely discernible as a monosyllabic query.

'You and the girl were fooling around with a game of seek and find. And it got quiet. You said.'

Clavell dragged a coat sleeve over his moisture-run face, nodded his head vigorously.

'Yeah, that's right. I called out Katy's name, but she wouldn't answer. For a while I thought she was still foolin' around. Then I had this kinda feelin'... I don't know. A feelin' somethin' was wrong.'

He shrugged, swallowed hard again. 'I guess like I had just now. God, Mr Steele, I'm really sorry. The way I acted after you'd taken the trouble to——'

'Borrowed time, kid.'

'Uh?'

'You were going to use your borrowed time carefully. Not waste it: especially now, when——'

'Yeah, that's right,' he broke in hurriedly.

Steele continued in the same even tone: '... the posse I didn't know was coming is almost here.'

He gestured with a gloved hand.

Clavell snapped his head round, peered out the window: saw the small, group of riders Steele had glimpsed from his new vantage point beside the stove. Let out a groan of despair as he folded through a half turn, presssed his back against the wall. Wrenched his head around to peer at Steele with renewed terror, his face drained of colour beneath the burnish. But there was no accusation in his eyes now. His hands clenched into fists, were caught in the same paralysing grip that trapped the rest of his being.

'Please... Help me?' The rasped words hardly scratched the silence. 'Honest, I didn't mean to...' He licked his lips. 'I just don't know what come over me, Mr Steele.'

The Virginian growled: 'It was a cup of coffee.'

7

Davy Clavell's head swung rapidly from side to side, his teeth gritted to keep them from chattering, his terror-filled eyes switching from Steele to the slow-riding group on the track between the crop of fields and back again. For stretched seconds as the silence in the wake of the Virginian's sardonic remark grew heavier with tension, the youngster once more looked close to cracking up into tears.

Until he found his voice, complained bitterly: 'This ain't no time for jokes, my God!'

'My time's my own to do as I want with, Steele drawled. 'Yours is borrowed. From me as I recall.'

'So what d'you want me to do?' the boy pleaded desperately. His Adam's apple seemed to bob at the same rate his eyelids blinked.

'Take it easy. You found out just a while ago that getting into a panic gets me mad.'

Clavell's hands began to clench and unclench at high speed. He was able to keep his voice steady when he pledged: 'All right, I'll do my best to stay calm. Honest.'

'And you're going to listen to me, do what I tell you?'

'Whatever you say.' He sneaked another look out the window. Then backed the assurance with a vigorous nod. Repeated: 'Honest, Mr Steele.'

The Virginian jerked a thumb toward the rear corner of the room, beyond the stove. Said against the first faint sounds of clopping hooves and jingling harness brass to reach into the house: 'Get the hell out through the back door and make yourself scarce. Until I say you can come back in.'

'What if——'

'You hear me say to ask questions on my time, kid?' Steele pointedly craned his head to the side, peered out the window alongside where Clavell was pressed to the wall.

The riders drew inexorably closer along the track, the sounds of their approach swelling in volume.

'But——'

'All right. Be stupid kid. Go for your gun again. See if you can drop me before I——'

'I'm sorry!' he almost shrieked, thrust up his hands: fingers splayed, palms toward the Virginian in a gesture of total compliance. 'All right, I'm goin'. I'll wait for you. I'll be careful and——'

Steele cut in wearily: 'Just be gone. Until I tell you otherwise.'

He went toward the front door and Davy Clavell headed for the back one on opposite sides of the table.

The thudding of hooves on the hard-packed dirt of the yard served to cover any sounds of the rear door opening, closing behind the departing youngster.

As soon as he had seen this rear door fold back into its frame, the latch come to rest, Steele turned and swung open the front door. Counted upon the sight of him on the threshold to capture the attention of the newcomers. So they were less likely to catch a glimpse of Clavell if the kid was careless in moving away from the rear of the house.

'Steele,' Len Fallows greeted curtly as he and the six other warm-coated, fully-armed men reined their horses to a halt in a haphazard line out front of the house.

'Sheriff,' the Virginian responded, inclined his head a couple of times as he let his gaze range over the rest of the grim-faced men.

Most of them acknowledged his greeting in a similar manner. They were the O'Malley brothers, Jack and Jethro, Kenny Coggins and Pete Ryan: along with the Providence liveryman Harlan Grout and the newspaperman Huey Attrill.

They did not present the appearance of the kind of posse that would cause hardened criminals to worry over much.

But they looked more than adequate to deal with a running scared boy of sixteen.

Only the stocky, running-to-fat Grout attempted anything approaching an amiable smile. And this quickly slipped from his ruddy complexioned face to be replaced by a frown to match those worn by the others, when Fallows announced:

'We have us a serious situation in the valley, Steele.'

The Virginian replied, even toned: 'I'm grateful you took the trouble to ride out and tell me about it, Sheriff.'

'Just listen to the man, why don't you?' This from the tall, muscular-bodied, hard-eyed Ryan. There was even aggression in the way he shifted his fat cigar from one side of his mouth to the other when he was through talking.

'Quit it, Ryan,' the barrel-bodied Jack O'Malley snapped.

'Yeah, shut up, Pete,' his just as bulkily built brother added, less forcefully.

'The Taggart girl got hit harder than any of us realised at first,' Fallows explained, fingered his bushy moustache while his dark eyes still glittered with the animosity Steele's response generated. 'Doc Mackay doesn't give her more than a fifty-fifty chance of coming out of the stupor that the blow put her in. And even if she does, he says there's a danger she may not be as she was before.'

'She could have brain damage, Mr Steele,' the slightly built newspaperman elaborated.

'Maybe have no memory left,' Harlan Grout added.

Steele sighed and replied: 'That's tough. I hope the coin comes down in the girl's favour.'

'There can be few people in the valley who aren't aware of just how *tough* you are, sir!' Huey Attrill pronounced. 'You certainly don't have to adopt such a hardened attitude with us. It's not what we hope you will——'

'Taggart's steaming mad, Steele,' Fallows cut in, directed a withering glare at the newspaperman. 'He's . . . Well, he's . . .'

'Demented is most likely the word for which you are searching, Len,' Attrill said, almost obsequious after getting himself on the wrong side of the lawman. 'Just like the whole town seems to be over this terrible business.'

'Shit, this whole thing is a waste of time!' Ryan snarled.

Glared at Fallows for a moment, then at the Virginian in the doorway. Went on in a disparaging tone: 'Seems certain people around here figure you're the cat's whiskers when it comes to trackin' sign and that kinda stuff, mister. That's why we're out here. Like I say, wastin' time.'

'Pete, shut the hell up,' Jack O'Malley urged.

'No, it's all right,' Fallows allowed, quite willing to have somebody else make the request which was the reason they were at Trail's End. To have done so himself would have stuck in his craw.

Steele eyed the most aggressive member of the posse with mild curiosity. And Ryan eagerly took up the invitation offered by the lawman.

'The Taggart guy is out for blood: the kid's blood. And he's stirred up a whole bunch of others to feel the same way. They ain't gonna wait around and find out if his daughter wakes up and tells what happened to her.'

He paused, rolled the half smoked cigar from one side of his scowling mouth to the other again.

Jethro O'Malley, in processs of tamping tobacco into the large bowl of his pipe, shook his head, said miserably: 'Reckon there ain't no doubt about what happened this mornin', Pete. Young Davy must've figured he got the come on from the girl. Lost his head. Panicked when she changed her mind.'

'I ain't disputin' it's what could've took place,' Ryan growled. 'That ain't no reason though for a bunch of guys to start a lynch mob. The girl'll maybe come out of it. The kid oughta get the chance to speak his piece in court!'

Len Fallows sought to re-establish his leadership of the group. 'That's about the sum total of it, Steele. The serious situation we have in the valley. Unless this legally constituted posse finds the boy first, and we take him into protective custody, Arnie Taggart and his bunch of hotheads will likely gun him down out of hand. Or string him up. Do any number of damn stupid things they'll all regret later. Like Ryan says, Clavell's entitled to the opportunity to tell what happened between him and the girl.'

'The Taggart faction have almost the whole town behind

them,' Attrill revealed grimly.

'Includin' most of the women, would you believe?' Grout added. Shrugged, allowed: 'But then, I guess, seein' what a boy did to a female that's about to be expected?'

Fallows had been peering fixedly at Steele as the additional details were provided. Now he looked to left and right, swept his questioning gaze over the men he had deputised. All of them seemed to consider the ground had been fully covered. Two signalled this with nods of confirmation. The others just tightened their lips to emphasise they had nothing else to contribute.

Steele nodded then. Asked of Fallows: 'You recall back on the trail, when we found the girl?'

'Yeah.'

'I said then if I ran into Clavell, I'd tell him what Arnie Taggart had in mind for him? And I'd do what I thought was best?'

'So?' Pete Ryan challenged, face contorted by a sneer.

'So nothing's changed,' Fallows replied sourly on Steele's behalf. 'Unless it happens he can't avoid it, he figures none of this is any of his concern.'

All eyes swung to become fixed on the Virginian. And the look on each face became progressively more contemptuous as the Virginian nodded his agreement with what the lawman had said.

'Didn't I tell you how he'd be?' Fallows asked rhetorically as he made a rapid survey of the posse, looked back at the man in the doorway. 'That reputation you have as a hot shot when there's trouble, Steele? These men who work with the kid, they've heard about it. They insisted we come out to see you. Against my advice. I told them what a changed man you figured you were.'

'I said you'd lend a hand,' Harlan Grout muttered, disappointed.

Attrill attempted to prod Steele into positive action: 'I'm sure we'd have a far better chance of preventing a tragedy if——'

'We all make mistakes, frig it!' Ryan snarled, snatched up

his reins in a way that emphasised his impatience to leave right away.

The skinny Kenny Coggins spoke for the first time. 'In makin' this one, I figure we've let the trail get too damn cold. Not that any of us was too sure we could follow a hot one, anyway.'

Jethro O'Malley at last succeeded in getting his pipe to draw to his satisfaction, spoke in dull tones around the stem clamped between his gums: 'Least we can try. Owe it to the kid.'

'Luck to you,' Steele said as the others took up their reins. Just when boiling over coffee began to hiss on the hot stove again.

Harlan Grout spat to the rear of his horse and muttered disconsolately: 'We're sure gonna need a whole lot of that.'

'No more than Taggart's lynch mob,' Huey Attrill pointed out.

'It's Davy Clavell needs it most, is my opinion,' Jack O'Malley said grimly, eyed Steele like he was vastly disappointed in him. 'Guess the kid ain't so much. But he ain't had enough time to amount to much.'

'We've talked this out, so lets get out of here,' Fallows said, tugged on the reins to wheel his horse. And the others did likewise as the lawman claimed: 'Didn't it turn out just like I told you men it would? Trying to get Adam Steele to change his mind is like battering your head against a brick wall.'

There was a buzz of disgruntled talk that was difficult to hear clearly against the snorts of horses, the clop of their hooves as the posse started off the yard. Also, each growling speaker competed with all the others. But the Virginian did discern some of the remarks were concerned with how the men would like to crack a brick over his skull: but because he was so hard headed it probably wouldn't hurt him.

He left the front door open when he turned, went to the kitchen area. Although he wore gloves, he made use of the same cloth as Davy Clavell to lift the bubbling-over coffee pot off the steaming top of the stove.

As he did so, he accidentally caught a glimpse of his grim-set profile in the mirror hung on the wall by which he shaved. He sighed, became impassive as he muttered, only just out loud to his reflected image:

'Feller, the way this thing is flaring up, you could get more than just your fingers burned.'

8

He poured himself another mug of coffee, carried it back to the open doorway. Where he leaned a shoulder against the frame, peered out after the departing riders who rode back along the track between the crop fields at the same slow pace as they had ridden in the other direction.

Some of them—never Fallows—directed over-the-shoulder glances towards the house. And then there were one or two double-takes as Steele was spotted again in the doorway: the mug of coffee he held seeming to stress his decision to stay here at Trail's End, not involve himself in the community's latest troubles.

Sharp words were exchanged, not loud enough to reach back to the house: and the order was given for the possc to move at a canter. So, even after they had gone from sight into the timber, the sound of pounding hooves marked the progress of the posse down the trail for a considerable distance.

While he slowly slipped coffee, reviewing in his mind his handling of Davy Clavell and the group of departing men, he heard no slow-down to a stop and a restart. Knew the men had not re-closed the gate after they rode on to the Trail's End spread. Certainly no-one took the time to dismount and fasten it behind them as they left the property.

Later, when just unobtrusive sounds of nature filtered out from the timber, Steele remained convinced he could not have handled this latest twist in the developing situation any other way.

For he had committed himself. Once he had gained the

trust of Davy Clavell and presuming, of course, the kid was still hiding out close by: waiting instructions from his mentor.

It would have been a whole lot better had he not returned home to find the fugitive kid hiding in the barn. Having done so, though, as a law-abiding rancher he could not simply have told Clavell to get the hell away from the spread. He would have had to turn in the kid.

Halfway through the second cup of coffee, he heard a series of small sounds from out back of the house that may have been made by the Fresian milker. But the sounds then culminated in a familiar tentative rapping of knuckles on the rear door.

Again Steele left the front door open as he turned into the house. The knuckles rapped a little harder. He said nothing, swung open the door. And Davy Clavell, in a state of high nervous tension, almost leapt away from the threshold. His mouth was starting to open to ask a question of Steele. It gaped to vent a strangled gasp of surprise before he could speak.

'God, I thought then...'

He squeezed his eyes tight closed. Only then, in the darkness behind the lids, did he realise fear had caused his right hand to go instinctively for his revolver. And he jerked the hand away from the butt of the holstered gun: fast as he had withdrawn it from the hot handle of the coffee pot awhile ago.

Steele told him evenly: 'No, kid. They all took off.'

'I heard the horses. But I couldn't see from over there.'

He was rooted to the spot where he had backed off. His eyes showed a lot less apprehension now as he jerked a thumb across the mound without a marker, already starting to merge into the landscape, where Billy Baxter was buried. Revealed he had hidden behind the end of the barn close to the creek bank.

'Heard most of the talk. I know you said to stay away until you called. But I just couldn't wait to get back to the house, Mr Steele. I... God, I don't know. I just can't seem able to stay still. It's much better for me when I'm——'

Steele emptied the coffee grounds from his mug, backed off

the threshold, instructed: 'Come inside, kid. Pour yourself another cup of coffee. Have yourself a cigarette if you can keep your hands from shaking long enough to roll one this time. 'I'll get the horses ready.'

'Horses?' Clavell was abruptly mistrustful, made no aggressive move but his stance and expression were challenging. 'Where we goin'?'

Steele told him wearily: 'Don't want to labour the point, kid, but I'm the one supposed to ask the questions.'

'Damnit, Mr Steele! I heard some of what them men from town and my buddies said! How they're about the only people around here who ain't plannin' to lynch me! I ain't gonna go any place unless I know there's no chance a lynch mob'll get their hands on me!'

Steele started to shake his head, then nodded, replied in the same weary tone as before: 'I was about to tell you awhile back what I had in mind. Taking you to Broadwater.'

'Broadwater?' Clavell chewed the inside of his cheek, nurturing doubt. 'Then what's gonna happen?'

'Tell you on the move.'

'Look, you been good to me!' the boy countered quickly. 'I can't deny that! But that don't mean I'm gonna do every damn thing you tell me unless I'm sure it's best for me!'

'Kid, I——'

'It's me that's in the big trouble and so——'

'Kid, you don't have the choice,' Steele broke in successfully this time. Showed a hard expression and spoke in a harsh tone that totally captured the youngster's attention. Continued in the same manner: 'I'm in the trouble with you now. I'm thinking as much of what's best for me as for you. So, you don't have the choice. I'm taking you to Broadwater.'

'But——'

'That time you borrowed could be fast running out. Fast as my patience, maybe.'

Steele turned and crossed the room, set down his empty mug on the table as he went by. He was about to step out through the front doorway when Clavell entered the house from the rear, asked:

'What d'you mean, Mr Steele. Time runnin' out fast?' He

was unaggressively afraid again.

Steele stopped, sighed, turned to grimace back at the anxious youngster. Then reached around the back of the door to take a sheepskin coat off the peg where it hung. Shrugged into it, picked up the Colt Hartford from where he had leaned it against the wall beside the doorway. Said in a tone that made it a query:

'You were scared when you found the girl and came here, I reckon?'

Clavell shook his head, whistled low, then answered tautly: 'I was scared near out of my wits, that's what I was.'

Steele nodded. 'None of Fallows' posse claims to be any great shakes at tracking. I don't know how any of the men who're riding with Taggart rate, because I don't know who they are. Much the same, I reckon. The kind of state you were in, though, I reckon you might have left plenty of sign it wouldn't take an expert tracker to pick up on. So, the quicker we make no tracks leaving here——'

'God, you're right! To hell with the coffee and smoke, Mr Steele. Can I help with the horses?'

'You saw the other saddle when you stowed my stuff in the barn?'

'Sure.'

'Bring them both. Saddle my gelding. I'll get one of the mares in off the pasture for you.'

He started across the yard toward the corner of the corral. The youngster stepped out of the house after him, cast a nervous glance toward the gap in the timber into which the posse had ridden. Then said quizzically, too loud to be involuntarily voicing a thought:

'Broadwater, uh?'

Steele heard, but pretended not to. Moved a short way out over the winter grass. He had schooled his horses well and all three trotted obediently across the pasture toward him in response to a shrill whistle.

He selected the mare which was smaller by a hand, left the second mare and the stallion to graze on nearby grass as he led the chosen animal into the corral.

Clavell remained silently preoccupied as he put the saddle

Billy Baxter had once used on the back of the mare. While Steele booted the Colt Hartford and checked how the kid had saddled the gelding, tightened the cinch a notch.

The youngster did not now spend quite so much time peering toward the point where the trail went into the timber. He glanced often at Steele, and the Virginian thought he seemed constantly on the point of voicing an entreaty for haste.

'Need a minute,' Steele said when he was through and Clavell was still fumbling with his chore. Then left him with the horses in the corral, crossed the yard to the house.

Inside, he scowled at the dark stains on the pine table from the coffee he had thrown at the kid. Then felt an involuntary grin drift across his face as he imagined what Arlene Forrester would have to say about this spoiling of 'her' clean place.

He cleaned up to the extent of putting the two mugs and the pot in a bowl. Checked the fire in the stove would safely burn itself out should he not get back in time to stir its embers to life. Closed the back door, then the front one behind him.

Saw Clavell had brought both saddled horses out of the corral, closed the gate on the mare and foal. Was astride his borrowed mare: sat the animal like a novice. Looked as nervously uncertain about the prospect of a lengthy ride as he was about the wisdom of everything else the Virginian had in mind for him.

'I'm grateful,' Steele told him, took his reins from the kid and swung up on the gelding. Explained: 'First we're going to take an easy ride down to the gateway. If we make it that far, we'll walk for awhile. In the timber. Pick up the trail to Broadwater north of the Timber Creek spur. All right? You ready?'

Clavell was about to voice an answer, then seemed to doubt he would be able to speak and also remain in control of the horse at one and the same time. He gulped and nodded.

'Fine,' Steele told him. Then showed a fleeting smile, added: 'Forget what I said about *if* we make it off the place. We'll do that I reckon. No sense in making it easier for the people who're looking for us. So stay quiet and stay alert.

Don't say a word unless you see or hear anything that strikes a wrong note you think I didn't notice?'

Another nod. Another gulp. Then the youngster decided he could trust himself to stay in the saddle and uttered a simple: 'Yeah. Thanks Mr Steele.'

'You're welcome. Let's go.'

Steele took the lead. He suppressed the impulse to direct more than an occasional glance over his shoulder during the first fifty yards or so. By then he was satisfied the boy was not an absolute beginner at horseback riding. Maybe anything more than the docile mare would have been too much for him to handle: but with the pace at a gentle walk, Clavell soon gained in confidence. Did not sit so ramrod stiff, nor clamp in his knees so rigidly, screw the reins up in tight fists.

He got no sense of satisfaction from making progress as a rider: but he was in no frame of mind to relish anything.

Off the track between the crop fields, moving through the timber, his mood became dejected again. On the infrequent occasions Steele turned to look at him, it was invariably to catch the kid hurrying to re-arrange his features. Out of the apprehensive frown with which he had been peering to either side: trying to penetrate the flanking trees as far as he could. While he strained his ears to pick up any sound outside of those made by the horses and the wild creatures that did not quieten at the incursion of intruders into their domain.

Like Steele had guessed, the gate in the boundary fence was open. When the boy and he were through, he dismounted, closed and securely fastened it.

It just happened he was fixing the gate when Clavell got down from the mare: had not purposely looked away to avoid embarrassing the kid. Who dismounted clumsily, twisted his left foot in the stirrup, could have been badly hurt if the mare had been skittish from mishandling.

Clavell reddened, explained sheepishly: 'I'm city born and raised, Mr Steele. A New York orphanage. Never did get to ride a horse until I moved out here, for the job with the telegraph company. Three months ago. Since then I mostly got to ride on the wagon anyway.'

'For awhile now we walk,' Steele reminded him, gestured with a gloved hand.

Then he went in the direction he had indicated and the boy followed. Splashed through the ankle-deep water of Timber Creek, struck off into the timber. Angled away from the strands of barbed wire strung between convenient trees and an occasional fence post that marked the south boundary of the spread.

The going was not easy, for they covered ground it was unlikely any man had trodden before. Few animals, either, large enough to trample any kind of pathway through the undergrowth of the forest floor.

So it took a disproportionately long time to cover a comparatively short distance. It was often necessary to take care where they set down their feet, to keep themselves and their horses from tripping on hidden tree roots. Sometimes it was necessary to backtrack, make time-wasting detours when they came up against thick clumps of briar blocking the shortest route.

They reached the major obstacle of the Providence River at a point where it was some fifty feet wide, slow-running between steep banks. But after they made their way a hundred or so yards north-west, around a curve in the river, they located a length of bank where, with care, they were able to lead their animals down a not so steep, rock and dried mud slope into the water.

Had he been alone, Steele would have mounted the gelding, ridden across a diagonal course toward a shingle beach on the opposite bank. But he was unsure of both the mare and Davy Clavell in this situation.

He began to wade out into the river.

'God, it's cold,' the boy said with a shudder when they were out far enough for the water level to be above their knees.

'Freezing to death is about the least likely way you're going to get it, kid,' Steele reminded. Tempered this with a grin which he thought was probably as cold to look at as the water was to feel.

'Right now, drownin's most likely, Mr Steele. I'm no better

at swimmin' than ridin' a horse.' Maybe his teeth chattered only from the cold.

'If it gets that deep, grab hold of the saddle, hope the horse follows mine. And keep your head out of the water. Don't panic.'

The advice was unnecessary for at the midway point in the river crossing, the water was only waist deep, and still clear enough to see down to the rock strewn bed. Less than two minutes later they were out of the river, shivering as they crossed the narrow strip of shingle and went into the timber again.

On the obstacle-strewn forest floor in the dappled shade cast by the mostly leafless trees, it was probably not much colder than out in the open sunlight. But they both shivered more violently, felt chiller than they had even when they were waist deep in water.

They emerged on the Broadwater to Providence trail at a point Steele thought was less than a mile north of where the Timber Creek spur cut off. It had taken over an hour to get this far, but to Steele it seemed much longer in terms of how bone-deep weary he felt.

The kid looked in a lot worse shape than the Virginian as they leaned against tree trunks. When he sensed Steele watching him curiously, he showed a brief, wan smile, offered:

'I ain't so sure that what Katy's old man has in store for me won't be easier to take than freezin' to death, Mr Steele. And I sure do feel like that's what happenin' to me right now.'

He shuddered from head to foot, looked down at the lower, sodden half of his clothes. Blew noisily into cupped hands, then hugged himself. The smile was gone by then and he looked miserable.

'Sooner we reach Broadwater, sooner we'll get warm, kid,' Steele told him, straightened from the tree, swung astride the gelding.

Mentally numbed and physically drained, Clavell no longer cared about demonstrating his lack of horsemanship. He clambered clumsily into the saddle on the patient mare at the second attempt.

'I'm ready, Mr Steele.' He looked as dejected on the horse as when he leaned against the tree. His tone was as despairing as his expression and slump-shouldered posture. 'And I don't just mean to ride. I mean I'm good and ready to have you turn me in to the law up at Broadwater. And not only to be in a nice warm cell, either.'

Steele heeled the gelding forward, signalled for the kid to ride beside him. When they were side by side, he answered: 'It's the way it has to be.'

'I know it.' He hung his head and in his present dispirited mood seemed much younger than his years. Then he vented a low grunt, raised his head to direct a frown of determination along the trail. 'Worked it out while we were cuttin' through the woods. There ain't nothin' else to be done. The Broadwater sheriff, I guess he won't allow Katy's old man to get near me. But maybe that Providence lawman wouldn't be able to hold out against his own people. So many of them. And, like you say, it'll get you off the hook, too. The way it should be, right?'

Now he looked at Steele who, after a nod and a pause, asked:

'You've decided against making a run for it?'

'Uh?'

Steele shrugged. 'Out in California any way but west there's a lot of country to run to. I reckon you must have given it some serious thought?'

'Yeah, I did, Mr Steele. But it ain't such a big country as it used to be.'

He gestured with a hand to the sun-glinting wire strung between the poles spaced along the east side of the trail.

'I know that from workin' for the telegraph company. I seen the maps they got of where the wires go to. Don't take but a few minutes for messages to get to most parts, the telegraph wire goin' so many places like it does these days.'

The Virginian said: 'I was hoping you'd have a better reason for not running than that, kid.'

'Uh?' Clavell had started to withdraw into introspective thought, was perplexed for stretched seconds. Then grimaced at Steele. Gave an emphatic nod, growled in a resolute tone:

'That's damn right. I sure do have. The best reason. I didn't do nothin' bad to Kate Taggart, Mr Steele. Ain't nobody believes me right now. If I run, I can't expect anyone to ever believe I'm tellin' the truth about that.'

'You want me to be the first to believe you?'

'What?' he blinked, swallowed hard. Looked more confused than ever. 'But I thought you did? Why else are you helpin' me the way you are, Mr Steele?'

'Before the posse showed up, you didn't get through telling me everything that happened after the girl ran off.'

Clavell's grimace deepened, but altered in the emotion it expressed as he delved into the dark recesses of his mind again: reaching back over troubled times to memories of the scene in the house at Trail's End. Then:

'Oh, yeah! I was tellin' you about this feelin' I had somethin' was really wrong? That where I got to?

'That's where you got to.'

'Well... Yeah, then I heard a wagon comin'. I was some ways off the trail by then. After I'd chased after Katy while she was foolin' around.'

'The company wagon?'

A shake of the head. 'No. Me and Katy, we'd gone north from where the gang were workin'. This wagon was comin' down the trail from the Broadwater direction. I didn't see it. Didn't try to. Just kept on lookin' for Katy. Still had that bad feelin' about somethin' bein' wrong. I didn't yell loud again until after the wagon went on by. The longer it was she didn't answer, the worse the feelin' got. And I didn't want nobody else to know nothin' about us bein' out there in the wood. Then I found her.'

He looked toward the man riding beside him and the power of his gaze caused Steele to turn his head. He saw the depth of feeling in Clavell's clear blue eyes as the boy pleaded:

'That's the absolute truth, Mr Steele. I saw her lying there in the grass. Her dress was torn. Showin' her... Well, Mr Steele, I swear it to you: I ain't never seen no female parts that way. Except in some pictures some other boy had at the orphanage when I was little. Pete Ryan, he wanted to take me to a cat house in Broadwater the time we stayed there when we started to bring down the wire to Providence. But I never went in that place with him.'

'I believe you, kid,' Steele told him and saw the relief this brought to Clavell.

'She looked dead to me. Had this big lump on her forehead . . .' he touched with fingertips a similar spot on his own temple. 'I didn't see her breathin', but I guess maybe I didn't stay around long enough to be sure of that. I just run, Mr Steele.'

He was starting to talk himself breathless and took a few moments to recover. Then continued in a monotone: 'I was in a blue funk, just like you said I must've been, that's for sure. But I guess I had enough of my wits about me to know I'd be sure to get the blame for what was done to Katy.

'Happened to come out on the spur that goes to your place. Didn't know it then, though. I got to the gate and climbed over it. Then I run some more. Saw the house and the barn with the doors open. I knew I had to rest up for awhile. Until dark, maybe. I don't know. Then run far away. Far as I could get.

'I circled around behind the house. I figured no-one was home. Hid in the barn. Then I seen you comin' on home and I——'

'Easy, kid,' Steele told him.

And in the vocal silence after Clavell had ended the final rush of his explanation, they both heard the clop of hooves and rattle of the turning wheels of a wagon rolling slowly toward them: heading down the trail from the Broadwater direction.

Steele immediately reined in his horse and Clavell did so a moment later. And after he had shot a frightened glance at the Virginian, the boy joined the man in gazing fixedly at the point where the wagon would soon come into view around a curve in the trail, two hundred feet or so north.

Clavell croaked from out of his arid with fear throat: 'Mr Steele, what d'you think?'

'I think you should get lost, kid,' the Virginian growled, gestured with a gloved hand to the closest area of cover in the timber flanking the trail. 'Just for awhile.'

He heeled the gelding forward. Briefly interrupted his concentration on the way ahead: turned and looked back at Clavell. Who appeared more frightened than he had been since he stared out the window at Trail's End, saw the posse approaching.

'You hear me, kid?' Steele rasped, gestured with an angrily emphatic motion of his hand for the petrified youngster to go into hiding.

And this time the degree of Clavell's fear seemed to clear his mind rather than throw it into a turmoil of panic. He half fell, half climbed from his saddle. Led the mare by the bridle off the trail, into the timber. A moment later was gone from Steele's sight, which meant he was certainly hidden from the driver and passenger on the seat of the buckboard as it came out of the bend on to the straightaway.

The driver was a woman. Tall and thin, at first impression looking wearied by the years she had lived as well as the miles she had travelled. Another first impression was that the almost as tall, equally as skinny boy hunched on the seat to her right was related to her.

By the time the wagon and the rider had drawn close enough for Steele to tip his hat, the woman to call a greeting, he had tagged them as mother and son rather than the older sister-younger brother they might have appeared at a distance. For the emaciated woman was the far side of thirty and the tall for his age boy no older than ten or eleven.

'Good afternoon to you, young man!'

'You get your hands high!'

The boy issued the command as he brought his own right hand up from where it had been draped over the back rest of the seat. Levelled a Smith and Wesson Russian at Steele. Steadied the aim of the revolver with his other hand as the woman suddenly reined in the two horse team to a jolting halt.

The look on her careworn face became a harsh scowl as she started to snarl: 'Don't be a——'

Steele reined in his horse. Again had to consciously suppress an impulse to look over his shoulder toward the spot where he knew Davy Clavell had disappeared from sight. He spoke loud enough for his voice to carry back that far.

'It's said kids should be seen and not heard. I hold that with some kids it's best I don't see or hear them!'

He had trapped the woman's still angry gaze with his ice cold eyes. Only when he had finished the harshly-spoken warning did she feel able to wrench her head around. Direct her fear-triggered rage toward its intended target. At the same time as she jerked a hand away from the reins, grasped the gun by the barrel, tore it savagely out of the youngster's two-fisted grip.

'Don't be a crazy little fool!' she shrieked. Swung her attention back toward Steele. Fixed an imploring expression on her sunken-eyed, hollow-cheeked face flushed under the paleness, as she groaned anxiously: 'I beg you, mister! Please understand! My Tommy, he's not like——'

'There's something else they say about children,' Steele broke in, his tone still hard and cold.

The woman swallowed hard. 'Excuse me. I don't——'

'First, be grateful if you'd get rid of the gun, ma'am.'

'What?'

She had obviously forgotten she still held the gun, her skinny hand fisted tightly around the barrel. She looked at it in horror for a moment: abruptly flung it off the side of the wagon. It was still cocked, but it failed to fire when it bounced on the hard-packed dirt of the trail.

'But, Mom——' the boy began to wail.

'Reckon I can't avoid having to see you, boy,' Steele told him sourly. 'But I don't want to hear you again, understand?

'Please, mister!' the woman forced out of her constricted by fear throat. Either lost her voice, or her grasp on what she had in mind to ask. Then, in a rush: 'Tommy don't deserve to——'

The Virginian showed her a brief smile, moderated his tone to assure her: 'Easy, ma'am. That other thing about kids? Since you got rid of the rod, I reckon I'll spare the child.'

9

The woman's thin face showed a gamut of expressions during three stretched seconds, as in her racing mind she struggled to make sense of what Steele had said.

Then she decided it had been some kind of unimportant caustic comment, dismissed it as she hurried to explain: 'Tommy's gotten to be too protective of me since we've been left on our own, mister. He don't mean no harm. He's a good boy usually. A fine boy. I didn't know he had the gun hid behind the seat, honest I didn't. But——'

The boy, not taking his challenging stare off Steele's face, broke in grimly: 'Mom, how d'we know he ain't the one did that to the little girl?'

'Shush!' his mother hissed, sent a warning sidelong glance at the boy. But then she peered long and hard at Steele: finally shook her head, calmed her jangling nerves. 'No, course he's not Tommy. He's a full grown man and...'

'You ran into somebody who told you a boy's wanted for an attack on the Taggart girl, ma'am?' As he said this Steele could sense an almost palpable pressure of Clavell's gaze boring into his back.

The woman nodded eagerly, anxious to switch the subject of the talk away from her aggressive son.

Steele built on the foundations of his first impressions of the two. The mother was far enough beyond thirty to be close to forty. Taller than he was himself by some three inches, but weighing little more than ninety pounds. From the way her threadbare coat fit her frame so snugly, she had not undergone any radical weight loss recently. Likewise, if she had ever been anything but plain, there was no sign of former good looks left in her sparsely-fleshed, deeply-wrinkled, yellow-tinged face. Her angular features were dominated by slate grey eyes and were framed by hair that was greying from nondescript brown.

While the boy continued to eye the Virginian with deep suspicion, totally lacking in any degree of contrition, he looked capable of unleashing the same kind of short temper his mother had shown she possessed. This son she had borne late in life was a couple of inches shorter than she right now, but certainly would soon outgrow his mother during adolescence. He had the same colour hair as she did when she was younger. The basic bone structure of his blemish-free face was a match for hers. His eyes were blue, a shade darker than those of Davy Clavell. He had on a worse-for-wear knickerbocker suit under an open topcoat that looked to be an altered to fit hand-me-down. A too-large cap sat jauntily on the back of his head.

The woman was saying: 'That's right, mister. We met up with a bunch of men huntin' that monster. Led by the father of the poor child who was attacked.'

From the way in which neither mother nor son shifted their eyes away from him, Steele had to assume he only imagined he heard Clavell's sharp intake of breath from back in the timber along the trail.

The woman continued: 'I'm very much afraid if they find the boy he'll be very badly treated by . . .'

She shuddered, could not bring herself to voice her fears of a lynching.

'How far up the trail did you meet them, ma'am?' Steele asked.

'Why d'you wanna know for?' Tommy demanded.

Steele reminded flatly: 'I said for you not to be heard, boy!'

'Oh, yeah? And what'll you do to me if I——'

The boy glared defiantly at Steele. Was so intent upon drawing a response to his challenge he failed to realise his mother had come to the brink of losing her temper again. Only at the last instant did he become aware of what was in store for him. When her left hand streaked across in front of him, fisted around his right upper arm. And she swung him on the seat to face her. So she could land a sharp, back-handed slap to his cheek.

He vented a howl of pain.

Her voice, not loud but with a meaningful tone the child obviously understood from experience, cut through and silenced the cry. 'I've told you lots of times, boy! You be respectful to your elders. Or you get treated like the baby you don't figure you are no more!'

She would have out-stared him even if tears had not welled up in his eyes. He hurried to dry them with his coat sleeve before they could start to course down his cheeks: the left as red as the punished right, for shame now transcended pain.

'Two miles, maybe,' the woman answered, her anger back under control as she released her hold on Tommy's shoulder. 'You're from the town of Providence, too, I guess?'

'Short way outside, ma'am.'

'If you wanna go join the... Join up with the girl's father and the men with him, don't let me and Tommy hold you up.'

She took up the reins, and the final traces of hardness drained out of her haggard features. Steele suspected she was just a hairbreadth away from having her controlled rage totally submerged by a wave of remorse for the blow she had struck her son.

'I'm grateful to you, ma'am.'

He tipped his hat again, gestured for her to drive the buckboard on by. And now took indifferent note of the rig which was old but well maintained. The horses, too, were well cared for. The tin trunk and the two carpetbags that were the buckboard's only freight were far from new, battered by miles of travel to many destinations.

'As I am obliged to you, sir,' she broke in on his idle line of thought. 'For allowin' me to punish my son in my own way for his ill-manners.'

She flicked the reins and the two horses responded wearily, moving off at the same unhurried pace as they had been making before the halt.

The boy turned, leaned close to his mother. Cupped a hand to his mouth and her ear. Told her something that caused her to bring the rig to a standstill again.

She turned to look back at Steele, ask: 'We'd be obliged to you again if we could have our pistol back, mister?'

'Sure,' Steele said.

The boy made to clamber down off the buckboard, was pulled roughly back on the seat when his mother saw Steele swing out of his saddle.

The Virginian retrieved the revolver, saw it was as well worn as everything else possessed by the travelling mother and son. He returned the hammer to the rest, handed the gun up to the woman, advised:

'If you want your fine boy to grow up to be any kind of man, ma'am, best keep this some place he can't lay hands on it.'

Tommy made a disrespectful sound.

His mother showed a fleeting frown that was maybe meant to convey her response to both the boy's snort and the revolver. Then she quickly replaced this with a relieved smile as she accepted the weapon that Steele handed to her butt first. Pushed it into a pocket of the coat that was so inadequate for this cold time of the year.

'Maybe soon Tommy won't have to feel so responsible for the safety of his Mom, mister. We was told by the men huntin' the monster, his father's in Providence. Just a short ways down the trail from here, is that right?'

'Reckon something under three miles,' Steele confirmed. He went back to his horse.

The woman seemed strangely reluctant to leave now, like she needed to be assured of something before she did. She watched, anxious, as Steele got back in the saddle. Then the boy made to whisper to her again, but she refused to co-operate. Would not turn and bend her head to his face. Said absently:

'It's bad manners to whisper in company, boy.' Then, to Steele: 'Were you in Providence this mornin', mister?'

'Yes, ma'am.'

'So you can maybe back up what we were told? My husband and Albert Dean showed up in town about the same time the hue and cry for the child rapist started?'

'That's right, Mrs Pope.'

She nodded, and something close to a smile of controlled joy crossed her prominently-boned, unattractive face. 'Then Tommy really can soon get back to bein' a child again. Thank you, sir. Thank you so much.'

The boy, with the exuberance of youth, did not even try to suppress his excitement, urged eagerly: 'Come on, Mom. Let's get movin', before we miss my Poppa again.'

A flick of the reins once more encouraged the two-horse team to set off at a measured pace.

Tommy implored: 'We can go faster than this, Mom! Please!'

'No, boy,' she answered placidly. 'I told you, didn't I? This time we're goin' to catch up with your Poppa for sure. I just know it. There's no need for us to rush.'

With this exchange, mother and son seemed to draw up an invisible barrier around themselves and the slow rolling buckboard. Inside of which they were confident their family problem would soon be solved: and interference from outside was firmly excluded.

Steele thought he caught part of something Tommy Pope said: '... the stranger's clothes are all wet and...' But the subject was curtailed by his mother, and neither of them cast a backward glance toward the Virginian.

Within a short time another curve in the winding trail carried the buckboard out of his sight through the timber. He waited until the sounds of the rig were lost amid the other, less obtrusive noises of the valley before he raised his voice just a little above the normal level, called:

'All right, kid. You been lost long enough.'

While he and the Pope mother and son were talking, or since the wagon began to roll and drowned any sounds he made, Clavell had moved from the spot where he first went into hiding. He now emerged from the timber just thirty feet back down the trail from where Steele waited: looked as nervous as when they heard the sounds that signalled the approach of the wagon. He halted alongside Steele, made no attempt to remount as he rasped:

'God, Mr Steele! So Katy's Pa and his bunch are

someplace between us and Broadwater!'

'Good to know, uh?'

'What?' He was wide eyed with shock. 'That the people who want to lynch me are between us and where we wanna get to? Seems to me that ain't——'

'I reckon, kid,' Steele cut in evenly. 'If we know where they are, they shouldn't be able to spring any surprises on us. Seems to me. Has to be better than not knowing where the hell they are?'

Clavell chewed on the inside of his cheek, anxiously pondered this reasoning for a few moments. At last nodded and just a slight doubt remained in his eyes as he swallowed: 'Yeah, course it is. What a dope I can sometimes be, uh?'

'That's one of the troubles about being young,' Steele told him. 'Way you make up your mind before you've thought through what's in it. Called being impetuous. We've all been that. You want to get mounted?'

The youngster gave another of his emphatic nods. Then, maybe because his mind was occupied with other matters and he had no opportunity to worry about what he was doing, he swung smoothly up astride the mare this time.

Once in the saddle a slight smile with a trace of humour in it crossed his youthfully good-looking face as he said: 'I know bein' young has got a lot goin' for it, Mr Steele. But right now I'm lookin' forward to gettin' a whole lot older.'

He raised a curved hand to his throat and pulled a pained face, to demonstrate he was referring to the danger of being cut down in his prime by a hanging rope.

They started to ride and Steele said:

'I hope that for you, too, kid.'

Through gritted teeth, Clavell emitted a low whistle, muttered: 'Tell you somethin', though.'

'Tell me.'

'When that little kid pulled the gun on you? I sure aged a whole lot while I tried to figure out what I oughta do about that. But when you said about kids not bein' seen or heard . . .' He shrugged. 'Well, I figured you meant me?'

'I did,' Steele confirmed. Then added ruefully: 'It's something else that's making me start to feel old.'

'What's that, Mr Steele?'

The Virginian sighed, grimaced, drawled: 'It used to be the way the lawmen looked.'

'Uh?'

Now he grinned sardonically at the confused Davy Clavell, replied in a tone that was just slightly soured: 'Nowadays it's the jokers who pull guns on me are getting younger.'

10

There was no more talk for some time as the two riders pressed northward at an easy pace, both of them alert for another interruption of the normal sounds and sights of the timbered valley. An interruption which this time might signal a great deal more trouble than that represented by a mother and son searching for a missing husband and father.

Later Clavell asked if he might smoke and Steele said that would be all right. Then the Virginian saw it had not simply been anger at being the butt of jokes which caused the kid to make a mess of rolling a cigarette this morning. He was as inexperienced at this as horse-back riding and—if he was to be believed—with women. But he eventually succeeded in making the cigarette, after wasting enough tobacco to roll three. Afterwards showed he was better at smoking it than making it.

Later still, when the tobacco smoke had acted to settle his nerves, he was able to say without a trace of apprehension on his face or in his voice: 'When I was hidin' back there, I kept thinkin' it'd be best if we'd both ducked outta sight. But you're right, that's for sure. It's best we know where the lynch mob is.'

Steele responded with a nod.

'You've figured somethin' else out, I guess? We're maybe in between the Taggart bunch and the sheriff's posse, Mr Steele?'

'I realise that.'

Perhaps a full minute elapsed while, deep in thought, Clavell smoked the cigarette down to a butt. And Steele waited expectantly for the kid to reach another conclusion: which was signalled by a gulp then a groan. Before:

'Oh, my God! The posse on our back trail? They'll meet up with the woman and her kid and——'

'Right,' Steele cut in evenly as the boy's voice got steadily louder and his face expressed rapidly expanding fear. 'And there's a good chance they'll figure out it was me Mrs Pope and her boy spoke with. So it won't matter too much if one of those inexpert trackers happens to spot what's left of a fresh-smoked cigarette on the trail.'

Clavell looked down at the short butt with the same kind of horror the Pope woman had peered at the revolver Steele returned to her. Then he grunted, angled his horse to the side. Nipped out the glowing tobacco embers and threw the dead cigarette end into a patch of brush. Claimed defensively:

'But it was you said it was all right for me to smoke! I guess the sheriff knows you don't and——'

Steele interrupted the frightened youngster: 'I also just now said it won't matter about that, kid. If Len Fallows and his posse find out from talking with the woman they're on my trail, I reckon they'll guess I'm not out taking the January air. And the sheriff for one will be certain I'm up to no good in his book. So I'll be grateful if you don't talk so loud. Wouldn't want anybody to hear you before we have the chance to hear them.'

Clavell groaned softly. 'Oh, God! Them or the others. Like I said, a dope!'

'But you're young enough to change your ways,' Steele said, his tone a little rueful again.

'Young enough, maybe,' came the grimacing response. 'Long as I get time enough.'

'Yeah,' Steele said, barely aloud. Like he heard something was said to him, acknowledged the remark without comprehending what it was. This as he withdrew into a world of private thought.

A little later, Davy Clavell became aware of the Virginian's pensiveness as he emerged from a period of introspection morbidly concerned with the violent death that threatened him. He glanced sharply at Steele, then peered around in intense concentration. Looked at and listened to the virtually unchanging scene: the hard-packed trail winding between towering trees which rose up out of the grass and brush covered valley floor.

Then he asked tensely: 'You heard somethin', Mr Steele?'

The Virginian eyed the youngster with surprise for the new fear he saw in his face.

'It's just you looked kinda ... Like you were——'

Steele shook his head, said: 'Sorry, kid. I was thinking of other things.'

Now he pointedly listened to the pastoral peace that hovered in the chill winter air beyond the sounds made by the two horses. Heard only the rippling of running water as the trail and the Providence River curved toward each other. But did not come close enough for the glint of water to show through the intervening band of trees. Then he said to the anxious youngster, without being sure if it was the truth or not:

'Reckon I've lived my kind of life for long enough so I can have other things on my mind without falling asleep on the job.'

After he faced front again, he sensed Clavell continued to study his profile. Knew the boy was about to question him, maybe voice his doubt about what he had claimed. He was finding it increasingly easy to read the boy's thoughts from his expressive face. Which, right now, did not cause him any sense of achievement. For he was primarily concerned with the disconcerting feeling Clavell was likewise able to look into his mind. And was just as doubtful as was Steele himself about the truth of his contention.

He spoke before the youngster could come up with a form of words maybe designed not to offend him, admitted: 'Or maybe I can't do that anymore, kid. A man gets older, he can only get any better at the talents he practises, I reckon.'

'That figures, Mr Steele.' He paused, pondered for a few stretched seconds, added: 'I guess what you're sayin' ... This is the first time in quite a while you've had to do somethin' like this?'

Steele told him evenly: 'These days I'm a horse rancher.

Been quite a while since I wasn't.'

'I know what you were before. They talk a lot about you in town. Some of the Providence people.'

'It's a quiet town. Not too much happens that's worth talking about.'

'Yeah, I know that. When things do happen, though—since you been around—you've took a hand. Some say they're grateful for that. And everyone else oughta be grateful. But there's others, though, say you're mostly the reason for the trouble that happens.'

'Yeah, kid. And I know that.'

'Now you've took a hand again.' He looked contrite as he added: 'And I'm real sorry it's my fault you had to.'

Steele corrected tautly: 'I don't have to do anything, kid. Unless I choose to.'

Even as he said the words, he knew he had no confidence in the premise.

'But if I hadn't finished up in your barn, you wouldn't——'

'My barn is where you showed up, kid,' Steele cut in. 'Far as I'm concerned, you're going to finish up in a cell of the Broadwater law office. After that, I'm through with you.'

'Why, Mr Steele?' He sounded genuinely interested instead of perturbed.

'Because what happens to you after that, you're not my concern.'

The youngster shook his head. 'I didn't mean that. I mean, why did you make it your concern in the first place? You never believed me until I was through tellin' you the whole story, you said. You'd already started to help me before that.'

'I didn't say I believed you then,' Steele reminded the eager-to-understand boy. 'I said I believed you didn't go to the Broadwater whorehouse with Ryan. No point in you lying about that: so I believed you.'

'So why didn't you——'

This was the problem which had occupied Steele's mind while he was apparently—or maybe actually—unaware of his present surroundings, the possible dangers they held, as he and the kid rode up the winding, sun and shade dappled trail. He was about to make a curt, sour-toned response that it was no business of the kid: but then he acknowledged to himself it had as much to do with Davy Clavell as with himself. For the kid was the subject of his object.

'——send me packin' right at the start, Mr Steele?' the boy had completed. Now waited with patient but intense curiosity for a response.

Steele seemed for several seconds like he did not intend to reply. Then: 'Like I said, I'm a horse rancher. I planned for all that other stuff you heard about to be put behind me. Every day I'm at Trail's End, doing what I want with my life, it ought to get further behind me.

'But the spread isn't a thousand miles from the nearest neighbour. I have to be part of the community I live in, kid. I'd sure like to cut myself off from everyone else in the Providence River Valley when I'm out on the spread and there's trouble. But I've decided I can't do that. Or maybe it was decided for me.'

'But, Mr Steele——'

'If you want to hear my answer, listen. If you don't, don't listen. Keep quiet until I'm through, all right?'

He did not turn to look at the youngster. Paused for long enough to be sure Clavell would not insist yet on saying his piece. Then continued: 'When trouble gets brought to my door—one way or another—reckon I have to take a hand.

'Mostly that means picking a side. It's the one I want to pick, maybe, but I can't usually go my own way. This time, I figured I could. Reckoned it was best to get you out from between two sides. Because, as you figured it, kid, Len Fallows—who wants to handle it the right way—maybe won't be able to hold out against Taggart if he's got so many townspeople on his side.

'And whether you're guilty or innocent, it wouldn't be good for Providence to have the people there scrapping for your neck like dogs over a bone.

'It especially wouldn't be good if Taggart's side won. Guilty or innocent, a lot of folks who don't have youth as an excuse would likely act impetuously. And regret it.'

He looked at the rider beside him now, as he concluded: 'So, kid, it's not for your sake I'm doing what I'm doing. It's for the good of the community I've chosen to settle in. And if that sounds crazy, or half-cocked, or high flown, or whatever, I can't help it. It's the reason I'm doing what I'm doing.'

Although he had been answering the youngster's questions, he thought they both knew he was really speaking aloud his thoughts. To get it clear in his own mind exactly what he was doing out here on the trail this bright, chill new year afternoon. Heading to Broadwater with a fugitive. A sheriff's posse in back of them. A lynch mob up ahead. When, in a perfect world, he would be back on the spread, taking care of Trail's End business.

Having talked it out, he was now sure he had it straight in his mind: felt he had justified to himself the time he was spending this way. Along with the risk he was running in the short term of antagonising those neighbours in the Providence River Valley who he sought to protect from the disturbing results of their own actions: should they have the chance in the heat of the moment to unleash such consequences.

Then Clavell showed, understandably, he was still more concerned with the trouble on a more personal level. When he asked dejectedly: 'So you still ain't sure if you believe me, Mr Steele.'

The response came automatically to the Virginian's lips. 'What I've said, kid: as far as what I'm doing is concerned, that doesn't matter a damn to me.'

The boy thought about this for many silent moments. Long enough for the lack of a counter to cause Steele to look at him. And then he saw Davy Clavell's expressive face convey by turns he was on the verge of breaking into sobs of misery or of giving vent to embittered anger.

He ended up on a middle course. Tears rose and glistened in his blue eyes as he snarled: 'So the hell with you! Thanks for nothin', you hardbitten sonofa . . .'

His sense of rejection by the man he had trusted to believe in him made the tears spill down his cheeks. And the shame this aroused in him triggered a brand of rage far more powerful than any degree of fear he had so far experienced since Steele had first seen him.

A moment later, he controlled his emotions: looked much older, much stronger, much more certain of his ability to guide his own destiny.

He thudded his heels into the flanks of the mare. Hunched his body low in the saddle as the horse lunged into a bolt, galloped up the trail on a course of her own choosing rather than responding to any instructions the boy endeavoured to give. If, indeed, Clavell had the opportunity to even consider a command to his mount while he clung desperately to the saddle.

A curse ripped from between Steele's compressed lips. Then he formed his mouthline into shape to vent a piercing whistle. But the mare did not hear the signal. Or was so incensed by the abrupt demand for speed from a rider whose emotional turmoil she sensed, she forgot her careful schooling.

The Virginian curtailed the sound, started the gelding less forcefully into a gallop. Half as wishful thinking, half with a cynical belief it was the most likely end to the headlong dash, he visualised the inexperienced rider and the panicked horse parting company. Saw in his mind's eye Clavell hitting the ground hard enough to break his stupid neck before the lynch mob or a legally appointed hangman could get a rope around it.

While he thought briefly along this grim line, Steele was just as conscious of the danger to his mare. He had paid good money for the animal less than a year ago. Spent more dollars on feed supplements to grazing. Had not yet had the opportunity to recoup any of the expense by breeding from her.

He spoke aloud, but did not waste his breath with shouting the threat as he emerged from a bend, glimpsed Clavell racing the mare around another, perhaps a hundred yards ahead:

'You injure that horse, kid, won't only be Arnie Taggart who'll be looking to lynch you!'

The thudding of hooves of the two galloping horses filled Steele's ears. The volume rose and fell at irregular intervals, dependent upon the thickness of the timber that intervened between himself and the kid astride the mare.

Sometimes he saw his quarry for several seconds at a time, on straightaways or long and sweeping curves. And whenever he did, he realised the prospect of Davy Clavell being unseated from his mount got more remote with the passing of time. The animal, though moving as fast as ever, was no longer in the grip of blind panic. The rider had control, through the reins and his feet. And the horse now responded eagerly to commands, relishing the exercise of a flat out gallop on a chill day.

The kid had sufficient confidence to cast an occasional backward glance when he heard in the change of tone of the hoofbeats his pursuer was in sight. But always too much distance separated them for Steele to read the expression on the youngster's face.

Knew his own features had run through a whole gamut of changes as his emotions switched: from impulsive hot anger, through resentment, bitterness, something approaching anxiety to an ice cold rage. Which at length he masked with impassiveness as he rejected recklessness: began to consider giving up the chase.

The reckless act would have been to angle off the trail: try to get ahead of the kid by cutting in a straight line through the timber while Clavell continued to swing around a wide curve. The timber had started to thin a little as the ground began to rise gently, the valley narrowing toward its head where Broadwater and the lake for which it was named were situated, some five miles distance. But there was still the risk of a hidden tree root or clinging brush bringing mount and rider crashing down.

If he abandoned the chase, there were alternatives to consider. He could slow down, keep heading north, find out what became of Davy Clavell. Or he could turn around, head on home, leave the kid to his fate.

The second course he rejected after just a few moments' thought: the decision not influenced by the alternatives it presented. Either to meet with the posse on the trail or to duck out of sight in the timber while Fallows and his men passed. Explain later, as he would surely have to, his part in Clavell's escape from the Providence area.

Firstly, the other course was best for the kid. Once he knew he was not being hotly pursued he surely would slow down. Take the time to realise he was galloping full tilt toward the lynch mob, making enough noise to warn them of his approach: give them the opportunity to set and spring an ambush.

And, also, there was the return of his mare to consider and this was best for that.

Steele was irritated with himself for not thinking it through to its logical conclusion at the outset. Because, he acknowledged with a grimace, he had acted impetuously.

He reined down from the gallop on a short straightaway, the boy in distant sight. Had neither the time nor the inclination to attempt a signal to the front runner as Clavell snatched a glance over his shoulder. Probably the distraught rider did not even realise the Virginian was slowing down before he lost sight of him.

After the sweating, mist breathing gelding was moving at an easy walk the sound of the galloping mare soon faded from earshot, without, as far as Steele could judge, slowing by a beat.

The Virginian briefly cracked his impassivity again. Expressed another grimace as he visualised an image of the Taggart bunch springing a trap to capture the boy: tried to convince himself he was primarily concerned the mare should not be brought down and hurt. But then he allowed his mind free rein and it concentrated solely on positive thoughts of the boy.

Saw Clavell slow the horse, angle off the trail, dismount. Either to tether the animal or lead it. Make furtive progress through the timber, secretly circling the lynch mob. To run for his life like he had said he would not: or to turn himself in to the sheriff at Broadwater.

Steele would prefer the kid to adopt this latter course. Firstly from a purely selfish motive: to get him off the hook of seeming to act against the best interests of law and order in the Providence River Valley. But, too, it would be best for the kid.

Steele had personal experience of being a fugitive wanted

for murder. In truth, he still was...

A gunshot cracked out and Steele abruptly reined in his horse, tried to keep his mind from racing over a whole range of images created by the sound. The report, of a rifle, came from a long way off in the north: but was loud enough to silence the wildlife in the surrounding timber. So total silence blanketed the Virginian astride the utterly still gelding before he stroked the animal's neck with a gloved hand, murmured:

'If that's somebody giving the kid his best shot, I sure hope his aim's as high as I reckon mine to be.'

Again, an impulse to hot anger grasped Steele. But this time he was able to hold himself back from the brink of reckless action. Remained as immobile in the saddle as the gelding was unmoving beneath him until maybe ten seconds had slid silently by.

Then a lone bird called. Others tentatively but with increasing confidence passed on the shrill message. There were some scufflings in the brush.

No more gunfire. No voices raised to disturb his immediate surroundings.

He heeled the gelding forward into another, far less frenetic gallop. And barred his mind to any thought it was likely to entertain in its present state: of anxieties concerned with his own immediate past, the present as it affected Davy Clavell, the future for both of them.

He erected a barrier to such futile notions by forcing himself to concentrate on listening and looking: honing the recognised natural senses and the mysterious sixth one to a sharpness he had not demanded of them for a very long time. Maybe for as long as he had been at Trail's End? But probably not...

Right here and now he was not in imminent danger. As he had been many times since he came upon the dying mother and her baby that had brought him to this part of the country. Up until that recent occasion when he was pursued as a killer...

He rasped a profanity, deeply irritated with himself for allowing his concentration to lapse: leaving his mind open to just the kind of thought process he had determined to bar.

But no harm had been done, unless to his confidence in his self control. No danger had shown itself. The only sounds were the beat of the gelding's hooves, the shrill calls of birds and, again, the rippling of running water. Running faster now.

Moments later he saw the Providence River when the trail emerged from a dense clump of timber to start to run parallel with the bank.

He slowed his mount, knew from riding to Broadwater before this was the start of a long, gentle curve of river and trail, a patch of thick timber on this eastern side, an expanse of rolling hills spread beyond the far bank. Low, grass-sided slopes featured with occasional outcrops of rock and small clumps of brush.

Here, just three miles from its source of Broadwater Lake, the river was narrower than where he and Davy Clavell had crossed it. Just thirty feet or so. But it flowed much faster between steep banks, broke white over jagged black and grey rocks.

So there had been no real chance for Davy Clavell to escape his fate by crossing these near rapids. And Arnie Taggart with the dozen or so men he had rallied to his lynching cause had obviously covered the other means of escape when they heard the galloping horse, set the ambush.

This at the far end of the curve of the trail, where the river ran out from a steep-sided rocky gorge, the trail continued its same arc that took it around the bluff on the valley bottom through which the river cut a course.

The men were clustered in a tight-knit group at this spot, some two hundred yards distant when Steele first saw them: immediately recognised Taggart from the way his coat draped the shoulder of the gunshot arm in a sling.

While he rode closer, again having to consciously suppress an impulse to speed, Steele thought he recognised most of the others. He was close enough to have his first impression confirmed when the cry he had been seen went up, for all the men turned to look toward him.

Harold Archer who ran the town's grocery store was in the group. So was Michael Morrison from the stage depot.

Martin Dyer, who had a small farm next door to Taggart's ranch. Abe Steiner from Mission Farm. Jake Lineker, whose daughter had set her cap at Adam Steele and was now dead.

Seven more to make it a thirteen-strong lynch mob. Five of the seven Steele was sure he knew by sight from seeing them in town, a couple of these by name. The other two were strangers to him, which did not have to mean they were strangers to Providence.

Their horses were still hidden from when the ambush was set. Just Davy Clavell's mount, Steele's mare, was out in the open, reins tethered to a clump of brush.

The kid himself was not immediately in sight, until the Virginian rode close enough to hear some low-pitched, discontented talk and the men shuffled here and there. Then he glimpsed a form sprawled out on the grass. Just beyond where the horse was hitched.

As they made their small movements and low-voiced comments, some of the men dropped hands to drape the butts of holstered revolvers. Others shifted rifles away from shoulders, canted them across the fronts of their bodies, switching from single to double handed grips.

'You better be ridin' through to Broadwater, Steele!'

The implied threat was voiced by Jake Lineker, a beefily built, almost bald, man of middle years with a thick black beard. Although he knew the Virginian could not be blamed for the death of his daughter, the farmer still nurtured a corrosive bitterness toward him.

'This here is a private matter,' Taggart augmented. In his element-burnished features there was a brand of calmness that starkly contrasted with the intensity of feeling showed by the rest of the men. Like, as the man most deeply affected by the tragedy, he experienced the greatest sense of quiet satisfaction at having captured the boy he was convinced attacked his daughter. 'Stand aside, men. Let him ride through.'

At first glance Davy Clavell may well have been dead. So still did he lay, face down. Then, as Steele ignored the commanding words and harsh looks directed at him, he saw the kid was breathing. And had his hands tied behind his back. Maybe was unconscious, petrified, or playing possum.

The Virginian reined in the gelding twenty feet short of the men, who gathered into a tighter knit group: not out of any sense of fear to seek comfort in closeness. Instead, in a concerted effort to protect their hard-won prize.

'I said——' Lineker started to repeat.

Steele fixed Taggart with an unblinking gaze, asked: 'There was a rifle shot, was the boy hit?'

Harold Archer, who was past sixty, balding, squint-eyed and walked with a limp, was the only member of the group to express any degree of shame at what was happening. He started to explain: 'It was just a warnin' shot, Steele. Get him to stop when we stepped out of the trees. And——'

'The little shit pulled rein so hard his horse went down and he was tipped out of the saddle,' the hand for hire Steele knew to be named Charlie Lacy growled.

'If it's any concerned of yours?' Taggart rasped. And his eyes now burned with the fire of the anger that raged just beneath the veneer of surface calm.

'He was knocked out cold, that's all,' Archer said.

'And now you're going to kill him?' Steele asked evenly. Made to get out of his saddle.

'Just as soon as the bastard wakes up so he'll know what's happenin' to him!' Taggart snarled. Hardened his voice still more to command: 'Stay on that horse, mister!'

The Virginian froze in the act of dismounting. Then swept a hard-eyed stare over every face, failed to provoke more than three or four of the men to waver in their grim determination to take a hand in Taggart's killing business.

Three revolvers slid smoothly from holsters. Two rifles swung to the aim. Here and there, hammers were thumbed back with a series of metallic clicks.

Steele said evenly without looking toward the group: 'Not so long ago I was concerned with which side to commit myself to. Sounds like it could turn out...' He completed the dismount against a buzz of harsh talk. When the talk ended, finished: '...to be suicide.'

11

The Virginian's back was still toward the men variously simmering with anger or torn by doubt. But he recognised the shrill tone of the short and wiry, leathery skinned Abe Steiner, raised to cut through the babble of tense voices.

'Don't be a fool! He'll kill you!'

All talk was stilled as Steele stood on the hard-packed dirt of the trail beside his horse. Other feet pounded the same strip of ground. And a warning bell sounded in his mind: it was to him the man who worked Mission Farm had yelled. So he checked the move to reach for the jutting stock of the Colt Hartford.

Turned just his head while his body remained toward the gelding: as the running man came to an abrupt halt.

Arnie Taggart stood rock still, legs splayed a little, less than ten feet away from the Virginian. The rancher's good arm was extended to its limit from the shoulder: pushed his cocked revolver that much closer to Steele's impassive face.

For what seemed like several stretched seconds, probably was just one or two, the tall and powerfully-built rancher seemed incapable of speech. While he teetered just a hairbreadth away from squeezing the trigger of the misused Remington.

Taggart's back was toward the lynch mob. But they did not need to see his hard set face. There was in the tension-crackling air, filled by the sound of rushing water, a quality that warned the men their leader was close to the brink of desperate action.

None of them moved. Maybe some of them held their

breath. All stared fixedly at Steele and Taggart: these two seemingly somehow detached from their surroundings.

Steele brought the brittle comments to an end, said in a flat tone that caused several gasps to be released: 'I don't want to die on account of the Clavell kid, feller. Don't reckon you'll want to live with yourself if you kill me?'

There followed another tense silence.

Taggart seemed not to have heard what the Virginian said to him: his mind perhaps in a turmoil of indecision concerned with how to deal with the unexpected factor of this man who was the sole obstacle to achieving what right here and now he most desired in the world.

Then his extended arm began to waver. The hand fisted around the Remington butt trembled. Steele broke out into a cold sweat, recognised the anguished rancher could now fire the gun in error. Should a twitching finger squeeze unintentionally against the trigger.

Which would be a stupid way to die.

'Mr Taggart, put the gun away!' Abe Steiner forced his tone down from the shrill height of a few moments ago. On his face was a frown of strain while his tone maintained the quality of reason when he tried to continue: 'If you kill Steele, I'm——'

'Blast the bastard with a bullet if he does anythin', Arnie!' Charlie Lacy urged. 'Or stand aside and let me break him in half if that don't have no appeal!'

Lacy was regarded as one of the hardest working hired hands in the Providence River Valley. Usually he was the most gentle of men, even though he had the kind of square-featured, element-burnished, narrowed-eyed and thin-mouthed face that provided the ideal backdrop for an aggressive glower. And was possessed of a powerful build that suggested he could easily back up what he had just said with deeds. A moment later looked like he would prefer to toss aside his Winchester rifle and try to do just this.

Harold Archer insisted: 'No! There shouldn't be anyone but the boy gets——'

'I said an old crock like you shouldn't have come along on——' It was the pallid-faced, red-headed, elegantlymoustached Martin Dyer who started to snarl the insult.

Was interrupted by the usually ineffectual Michael Morrison who rasped: 'Damnit, I'm with Archer! I didn't join up with this posse to see local folks get hurt!'

A man whose name the Virginian did not know made the sour-toned point: 'When Steele wants somethin' bad enough, he don't give too much of a shit who gets any lumps!'

'Shut up!' Taggart said. Not particularly loud, nor with any particular force in his voice.

So, maybe just because he was the accepted leader of the bunch, or perhaps they detected a subtle hint of danger in the quiet-spoken words, he was instantly obeyed. Then, as the sound of water rushing out of the gorge and hissing around the rocks filled the silence, he started to answer without need of further thought:

'I know what you said, mister.' He lowered his gun hand, eased the hammer forward, returned the Remington to the holster. In the time it took to do this, his eyes lost their intent to blast a bullet into Steele's head, showed an expression of understanding. In back of which was a desire that he, too, should be understood. 'I thank you for sayin' it, I guess. But I want you to know... What I'm goin' to tell you...'

'Shit, Arnie, let's——'

'Shut up, you damn fool!' Abe Steiner snarled at Lacy.

The glowering man shifted his hard-glittering eyes from Steele to Steiner and back again.

Taggart gave a curt nod of agreement with Steiner's sentiment. Did not switch his gaze from Steele's face, pressed on: 'I'm goin' to hang that boy who hurt my girl the way he did. Maybe killed her, even. Or if he didn't do that, made it so she won't ever be my girl again, not really.

'Just the one way I won't do it, mister. And that's if I'm dead before I get the chance. Want you to be sure to understand that.'

He showed a kind of mirthless smile that came and went across his face within a part of a second. Pointed out with something close to a triumphant note in his voice: 'So, mister, the boot's kinda on the other foot, so to speak? If you wanna keep me from stringin' up the Clavell boy, seems like you'll have to live knowin' you killed me?'

He turned slowly, without waiting for a response from the Virginian. For which Steele was grateful, since he had no ready reply to offer. So determined was the rancher's demeanour: so unassailable his position of strength from which to do what he wanted.

Taggart began to move resolutely back toward the men, and they parted to allow him unimpeded passage to where Davy Clavell lay.

Steele was made to realise just what kind of tight corner he had got himself into as Abe Steiner told him grimly:

'Far as I'm concerned, live with it is what you'll have to do, Steele. I sure ain't gonna have your death on my conscience.'

He had a rifle sloped to his shoulder. He pushed the stock forward and up, so the Winchester was parallel with the ground, resting across the top of his shoulder, pointed behind him.

Charlie Lacy tipped his rifle barrel forward from where it had been canted to his shoulder, brought up his other hand to cup it close to the muzzle. Snarled with a savage grimace: 'Frig that, Steele. You try to stop Arnie doin' what he's got a right to do, you'll be in hell ahead of the kid!'

Taggart was among the group by then, moving through the gap they had opened up for him. From the way he snapped his head around to fix the hired hand with a glare, it seemed to the Virginian it was Abe Steiner's view the rancher wanted to hold sway.

Taggart did not break stride. By the time he reached Clavell's side, rapid exchanges of looks and some low-spoken words had polarised the men into two factions.

Just Martin Dyer, Jake Lineker and the blond haired man unknown to Steele were aligned with Lacy. But although they had tightened their fisted hands around revolvers or on rifles, none brought his weapon to the aim.

Then Taggart halted, spun on his heels, looked back through the gap in the crowd, told Steele: 'I don't care, mister. I don't care about you. Or what these men plan to do to you. All I want is to string up this piece of——'

'He's your prisoner, Taggart,' Steele broke in, aware of the strain in his own voice as he sought for and knew he failed to find a form of words that would sway the man. 'Why does it have to be here and now you hang him? Why don't you wait until Kate comes out of it and——'

'Because——'

'Because Len Fallows and the kid's buddies will maybe get here by then and it'll be too late!' the blond-haired man put in.

Taggart squeezed his eyes tight closed. Clenched his fists. Was suddenly pale. Started to tremble. All this as he struggled to keep his temper in firm control. Like he felt he was just a beat away from losing his grip: and knew if he did there could be no return. And unless he was in total control of himself, he could not be certain he would derive the eagerly-desired satisfaction for which he craved.

Steele started: 'But what if you're wrong and——'

'I'm right, damn you!' Taggart yelled.

Lost control. Turned, launched a vicious kick at the boy. The act of a man who had been driven across the line into insanity at that instant he moved to the attack: landed a kick powerful enough to lift the inert weight of the boy clear of the ground, twice turn him over and thud him down on his back.

Davy Clavell's hung open mouth uttered only a forced, noisy expellation of breath as his body, limbs and head flailed in the manner of a rag doll.

So plainly he was unconscious, as yet not feeling the pain of Taggart's sudden viciousness.

Even before the boy came to a thudding rest, Steele was himself gripped by a kind of insanity. That drove him, perhaps, to react with a greater degree of recklessness than ever before. Unless it had happened some of those times in the War Between the States: when the heat of battle blinded and deafened him to everything except that to which, at the instant, it was vitally important for him to accomplish.

He swung away from the gelding, plunged forward. Toward the gap opened up by the men through which Taggart had gone.

Committed to committing suicide. This phrase raced constantly through his mind.

His determination when he dismounted from the gelding.

Challenged many guns to cover him, blast him into eternity. Which was an act damn close to attempting suicide. For it had required just one itchy finger to squeeze the trigger of a well-aimed gun.

Then the tense moments after the challenge and counter challenge between himself and Taggart. Each of them, then and there, not prepared to go further than issue veiled threats. But any one of the small group of angry men for whom Charlie Lacy was the spokesman might have felt himself pushed too far: squeezed his trigger in the heat of the moment.

Now, again, Steele was asking to get himself blasted to death as he bolted forward, unmindful of any kind of consequence. It just mattered that he should stop Arnie Taggart landing a second brutal kick against the defenceless Davy Clavell.

Suddenly, there was no gap: the men had closed it.

Steele attempted to swerve to the side. Go around the bunch of men, not one of whose faces he now recognised. Their features were only blurred images. Just, too, as he failed to comprehend one word out of the barrage yelled at him.

He forced himself to keep that single objective firmly lodged in his mind: all he wanted was to prevent the man connecting with a second kick. Knew, without understanding how he could be so sure, that should Taggart land the kick, the enraged rancher would be pushed over the brink into total insanity. Would kick the boy to death.

If Steele could draw the man's rage toward himself, just maybe——

But somebody else would have to prevent the mindless act of slaughter. Because a fist hit Steele in the belly and he doubled over, began to fall. Something smashed into his face: too hard to be a fist. The blow forced him to straighten. Then a chop to the back of his neck sent him forward again.

He bounced against somebody, but the man swung away. Steele was certain this was Michael Morrison, the man from the stage line depot, expressing horror. But at what, Steele had no clue.

Then it didn't matter: for now there was a gap in front of the Virginian again. But he had no chance to lunge through it. His feet were rooted to the spot, as if held there by some powerful adhesive.

Then they were swept from under him. He tried to reach forward with both hands, to break the fall. But somebody else's hand fastened over one of his forearms, tried to wrench the entire arm out of its socket.

Steele was forced into a half turn, and he jerked against the grasping fist, tore free. An instant later he fell hard to the side. Glimpsed Davy Clavell sprawled on the ground just beyond his reach.

Taggart stood over the boy, his stance non-aggressive now. And, maybe because of the disorientated state of his mind, Steele thought he saw something akin to remorse in the rancher's face. Or maybe, he thought, he saw only what he wanted to see.

He hit the ground, experienced a bolt of pain that threatened nausea. Certainly he tasted the acid bite of bile in his throat. Or maybe—he seemed to have lots of time to reflect—he was just sick with himself for yet again getting this deeply enmeshed in other people's trouble.

Davy Clavell's trouble...

Arnie Taggart's trouble...

The valley's trouble...

Shit, *his* valley's trouble...

Taggart roared: 'Leave it!'

But the rancher's cry was too late. Or the eager for violence man he yelled at refused to hear the command.

Something hard and heavy—a gnarled fist, a boot, a rifle stock or a revolver butt—thudded into Steele's belly. And the bright, chill day was immediately a pitch black, stiflingly hot night. His trouble was abruptly over and he was in no position to give a damn about those of anybody else. He thought.

But it was not to be.

He hurt all over and a buzzing filled his head. He chose to believe this could be the sound of his brain starting to function again. For against the background of this buzzing he worked it out he could not hurt *all* over.

He had been kicked, punched, clubbed with guns and maybe head butted. But he recalled he was on his feet and moving during most of that. Taggart had tried to prevent the final blow that seemed to pitch him into oblivion. So, after the moments or minutes of blessed unconsciousness came to him, Taggart was hardly likely to allow his divided followers to pummel the Virginian's body.

He felt relieved he had the ability to commence and sustain such a thinking process. Then, before he could begin the next stage, catalogue the areas and seriousness of his injuries, a piercing scream cut through the gentle buzzing.

He snapped open his eyes and the scream was at once curtailed. The buzzing changed key. He experienced a terror—such as that expressed by the scream—that he had vented the shrill sound. Then felt a greater flood of relief than before as he took a firm grip on reality. He had not made the sound.

He saw he was propped in a sitting attitude, back rested against a tree trunk, legs splayed out on the grass, in the vee between two exposed tree roots.

The buzz in its new form, out from under his skull, was the rushing of running water as the Providence River emerged from the gorge in the bluff, bubbled white among the rocks.

He tried to turn his head, but it threatened the now familiar sensation of being sick to his stomach. So he held his head rigid, moved his eyes back and forth to the extent of their sockets. Recognised he saw the river scene from much the same point as when he sat his gelding, made the dangerous dismount.

Only the river, the timber on this side, the rolling hill country beyond the far bank and the sky were as they had been then. He needed to crack his eyes to slits against the brightness of the unclouded afternoon sky and the sunlight reflected on the water.

Then he could focus with less pain on the scene of impending execution.

It was Davy Clavell who had vented the piercing scream. Just why the boy gave vocal release to his terror did not matter. Now he sat silent and moving astride the patiently waiting mare; within a sharp slap on the horse's rump of having his neck stretched. For his head was in the noose of the rope that at present hung, a little slack, from a high branch of a completely leafless oak.

Whatever fear had triggered the scream, it seemed to have drained Davy Clavell of the will to protest further. He was still afraid to die, but faced it calmly as he peered directly ahead, clear blue eyes unblinking, curly blond hair moving a little with a stray breeze from out of the river gorge: the expression on his evenly tanned, immaturely handsome face a kind of sadness.

Steele looked away from the kid. And his first thought was that if he had not arrived at this place of execution when he did, his coming acting to divide the lynch mob into two unequal parts, there would still have been the division now plain to see.

Charlie Lacy and the blond haired man stood near the disabled Taggart. Obviously they had undertaken the necessary chores of lifting the doomed boy into the saddle, fixed the rope to the tree branch, placed the noose around Clavell's neck. Steele's gelding, tethered to a thicket of brush nearby, had apparently been used to accomplish the final preparations for the lynching.

The expressions on the faces of these two men were of vicious eagerness. Probably they were the kind who gave little or even no thought to the guilt or innocence of whoever happened to be astride the mare. They were here just to see somebody die.

Arnie Taggart himself now expressed no relish for his chosen task of executioner. From the moment he looked down upon the violated body of his daughter, until he launched the brutal kick at Clavell, he had carefully nurtured this moment. Perhaps had used a constant image of the present scene to drive him on the search for Clavell. Kept his mind free of thoughts of his daughter. Off the moral issue of if he was right or wrong to take the law into his own hands.

Now he stood beside the mare, a little apart from his two prime helpers. The hand of his good arm massaged the back of the one that protruded from the sling. On his face was an expression akin to that which Steele thought, just before he was plunged into unconsciousness, might have been remorse.

But not remorse. Not quite regret. Doubt, anguish, grief, a kind of painful nostalgia for what once had been? All the things a good and decent man might feel when he is forced by circumstances to consider an act against everything he has been until now.

'Taggart! For pity sake, get it over and done with!'

Steele did not know who made the plea. One of the ten men who had been moved to join the lynch mob, many hours ago, many miles from here. Now they—including some who had remained eager to the killing until almost the last—stood in a huddled group apart from the doomed boy and his executioner, the two men who were grinning with expectation.

There was a ripple of movement through the group. Heads nodded. A murmur of sound. Voices whispering agreement with what had been said.

Charlie Lacy scowled at the group of faint-hearted men. Smiled brutally at Taggart when he urged: 'You take your time. The way things have turned out, you got all the time in the world.'

'Yeah, make the little shit sweat some, Mr Taggart,' the blond-headed man encouraged.

The troubled rancher swept his gaze toward the source of each voice, his expression becoming more despairing with each passing second. Then he peered up at the silent, immobile Clavell, like he expected the boy to speak.

But Clavell seemed not to be aware of being studied by the man below him. Perhaps he was not aware of anything outside his own numbed mind: so still did he sit, so fixedly did he gaze into the middle distance. Without seeing the river, the timber, the hills and the sky that filled the panorama. Nor the Virginian who was a feature of the scene.

'I'll say the same as before, feller,' Steele yelled. Drew all eyes except those of Clavell to him as he got slowly and painfully to his feet: would have stumbled back down again, he knew, without the solidness of the tree to lean on. This as the pain in his belly became worse than that at the back of his neck. But he refused to indulge the discomforts. Needed all his willpower to keep from throwing up as he added: 'All the time in the world will be a real long time to regret what you've done, Taggart!'

The Virginian was disconcertingly aware of the risk he ran. It was his first challenge which triggered the rancher into violence before. Now it could happen again. For Taggart's resentment at interference from anyone outside the lynch mob could be precisely what he needed to overcome his trepidation. Even though the Virginian had perhaps put into words just that trepidation which held him back.

Taggart could step forward, pull his nervous hands apart, bring the palm of his good hand sharply down on the rump of the mare.

For long moments as Steele made the effort to stay on his feet, Taggart eyed him across the intervening ground with another gamut of ever changing expressions crossing his face. Mild surprise. Apprehension, non-comprehension. A pleading for understanding. Melancholy. And the beginning of the kind of mask behind which Davy Clavell had withdrawn.

Like the both of them were spiritually detached from where they sat and stood.

In such a state, Steele realised with a sense of dread, just as Clavell was uncaring about what happened to him, so Taggart would not feel responsible for causing it to happen.

Steele alone heard the slow groan of despair from deep within his throat as he fought to push himself upright from the tree. Willed his legs not to buckle under him. Blinked rapidly against a suddenly far more intense level of dazzling brightness from the sky and the river. Felt sick to his stomach again as he acknowledged there was not a chance he could prevent the hanging now. Experienced the first awesome realisation that in taking the course he did at the outset he had been destined to have a share of the blame for the inevitable tragedy.

'Hold it, Taggart!' a familiar voice bellowed.

'If you friggin' don't, mister, you're dead!'

Steele knew he should recognise the second speaker, too.

As, once more, all eyes save those of Clavell directed their gazes toward him. But the Virginian suddenly had the disturbing feeling he was about to slip back into unconsciousness. For he saw all the shocked faces as if through a grimed piece of glass. Next he was struck by the equally unnerving notion this was all a dream. Such was the quality of unreality to the scene that had blurred in response to the unexpected intrusion of the harsh-toned voices.

But the unmistakable sounds of gun hammers being thumbed back abruptly acted to clear his vision. Then, the series of metallic clicks having been recognised for what they were, he fastened on the certainty that the command had been bellowed by Len Fallows, the threat snarled by Pete Ryan.

He next saw the men of the divided lynch mob and even the boy on the horse were directing their stunned attention to a point in back of where he stood beside the tree. Then dry twigs snapped, men's leg bones cracked, breath hissed out after being pent up for so long.

Steele's neck felt like it was broken as he twisted his head to look over one shoulder, then the other, to either side of the tree. Because of the bile the pain erupted into his throat he could not trust himself to speak when he saw aligned in the timber all but two of the men who had come to Trail's End.

All of them ignored him.

'We got a deal for you, mister!' the near toothless, squat-bodied Jethro O'Malley yelled anxiously. 'You give us the time to fix this up, it could maybe save two lives?'

'One of them yours!' the tall, broad, belligerent-faced Ryan added, talking around a dead half-smoked cigar clenched in his teeth.

This as Jethro stepped out from the trees on to the trail, held up a black box not unlike a doctor's bag.

'What is that?' Taggart asked thickly, his voice cutting across the buzz of talk started among the large group of his followers.

'A box of tricks is my bet!' Lacy snarled. Spat and scowled. 'It's all friggin' over now, Goddamnit! Didn't I tell you, get it over and done with before some other interferin' sonsofbitches like Steele get here to stick their noses in?'

If anybody recalled he had later claimed Taggart had all the time in the world, nobody voiced the thought.

The blond-haired man snarled, almost petulantly: 'Shit, there ain't gonna be no hangin'! Might as well go get our horses, head on home, uh Charlie?'

An instant later, everyone except for one man suddenly froze. All talk ended.

This as the rancher took a step toward the mare. Raised his good arm, hand splayed. For a stretched second, tension had a palpable presence in the cold air. Nobody dared to breathe. Until Taggart said, his voice as hard and embittered as the look on his face:

'Speak your piece, mister! But make it fast! I'm about run out of patience with this business!'

'Couple of the telegraph men went back to town——' Fallows started to respond quickly.

Taggart broke in harshly: 'The man with the box does the talkin'!'

Jethro O'Malley was suddenly disconcerted to be at the centre of attention. He swallowed hard, nodded several times, stepped further out on to the centre of the trail. Only now did Steele notice he was the only man on the posse without a drawn revolver or a levelled rifle.

'It's like the sheriff was sayin', mister. My brother and Kenny Coggins, they went on back to Providence. Finish workin' on bringin' the wire to town. Sure to have done that by now, I figure. So if you'll let us fix up this equipment to the wire . . .' He thrust out the box with one hand, jerked his other thumb up at the line strung between two poles immediately overhead. '. . . we can talk with Jack or Kenny in Providence. At the stage line depot. Find out how your daughter is, mister. If she's come out of it and——'

'Talk?' Taggart was scowling mistrustful.

'Well, in Morse, mister,' Jethro allowed, a little despondently. 'That's what's called a code and——'

'The hell with that!' Lacy snarled. 'It's a friggin' trick, I tell you!'

'Shut up,' Taggart growled absently, his hand still rock steady above the rump of the mare as his hard, flat, expressionless gaze remained fixed upon Jethro. While everyone—everything except for the relentlessly flowing river—responded to the order. So near silence filled the afternoon again. Until Taggart said: 'All right. But I ain't makin' no promises. I sure would like to know how my Kate is, though.'

Davy Clavell's mask of a face had flickered with concern for something beyond his own safety when O'Malley mentioned the girl. Now he even nodded in agreement with the man who was so close to killing him.

A sense of relief had encompassed the larger part of the lynch mob, as well as the posse. And Jethro O'Malley swayed, like he was close to collapse with this share of it: before he looked back over his shoulder. Swallowed hard, said:

'There you go, Pete.' He looked back at Taggart to explain anxiously: 'Pete or Kenny or the kid climb the poles, mister. I got too much weight for that kinda work.'

'Just get to doin' what needs to be done,' Taggart answered dully.

Ryan holstered his revolver, spread a grimace across his aggressively-moulded face as he stepped out on to the trail beside the older, shorter, fatter man: took the bag from him.

The other men who formed the depleted posse advanced out of the timber, some to one side of the tree against which Steele leaned, some to the other. All of them continued to keep their guns pointed in the general direction of the trio who stood near the mare. But none of the revolvers or rifles were carefully aimed now.

'You've made a wise decision, Arnie,' Abe Steiner said thickly.

This drew some low-toned words of agreement from the men around him, immediately silenced when Taggart growled:

'I ain't decided nothin' yet!'

The blond-haired man nodded emphatically.

Lacy said: 'Damn right!'

Davy Clavell's mouth worked as his gaze darted from O'Malley to Ryan to Len Fallows, to Harlan Grout to Huey

Attrill to Adam Steele. But just low, incoherent sounds emerged. Then tears spilled down his cheeks and he gave up the struggle to voice his gratitude. Fought not to lose control of himself.

Harlan Grout, to the right of Steele, switched his revolver from one shaking hand to the other and back again. Muttered: 'Man, you sure do look in bad shape. And I sure could use a drink.'

On the other side of the Virginian, the rifle-toting Huey Attrill murmured: 'I could use some faith this is going to work. even if Mr Taggart understood Morse, he'd be likely to suspect a trick.'

'That's right, feller,' Steele growled as Ryan hunkered down, opened the box, revealed a wood and brass telegraph key and some coils of wire. 'Unless Taggart trusts this particular code of the west, I reckon the telegraph will be sounding taps for Davy Clavell.'

12

The cigar-chewing Ryan required more equipment than was contained in the black bag and O'Mally went to bring it. Had to go back to where the posse left their horses so they could make a silent approach to this bend in the river. After he returned with a saddlebag, having spared some time to light his pipe while he was gone, Ryan needed just a few minutes to prepare himself and do what was necessary.

He used a leather strap slung around his waist, iron contraptions fixed to his boots with spikes protruding from beneath the toecaps, and well practised skill to climb quickly up the nearest telegraph pole. He played out a coil of wire behind him, the other end connected to the telegraph key which now stood, brass parts glinting in the light of the late afternoon sun, on top of the closed box.

Jethro O'Mally squatted beside the box, fiddling with the wire and the key like a man who had nothing useful to do but tried to appear occupied.

While these two men were busy with the mysterious technicalities of the telegraph the farmers and the ranchers, the businessmen and the lawman mostly watched the preparations in anxious or cynical silence. The sporadic talk there was did not carry beyond the men engaged in the exchange as more than incoherent mumblings.

The start of a bitter-toned discussion between Lacy and the blond-haired man was curtailed by Taggart who broke his grim-faced study of Ryan to glare them into silence.

Steiner, Lineker, Archer, Morrison, Dyer and the others in their group talked in undertones and from the expressions of some of the men it seemed they were hopeful it was all going to work out for the best.

Len Fallows, his face showing an embittered frown, forced Harlan Grout to step aside as he moved closer to the Virginian, accused: 'I figured you'd have a finger in this pie, Steele. Soon as I realised it was you the Pope woman met up with on the trail. Know it's not any coincidence, you being out here where the trouble is.'

Steele had started to feel stronger: strong enough to be confident he could now move away from the tree. To stand unaided without the reassuring knowledge there was something solid close by to lean on should he need it.

If he wanted to move away from the tree: but he did not.

Unless he could go across the trail, step down into the cool river. Stand waist deep in the water. Every now and then duck his head beneath the surface. So the water might sooth the burning sensations at his belly and neck. And he'd drink some of the water, too. To extinguish the fire the corrosive bile—now back in his stomach, thank God—had ignited in his throat.

But although he felt sure he could make it to the river, he knew it would be a stupid act. There were far more important considerations than his minor discomforts right now. So he had to be content to recall how the water felt when he and the kid waded in this same river for a far sounder reason. And to imagine how good it was going to be, back at Trail's End, to boil up some kettles and pans, soak his punished body in a tub of hot water.

'You hear what I said to you, Steele?'

The Virginian looked at the rough-hewn, sun-burnished, bushy-moustached, dark-eyed face of the lawman. And was in time to see a look of concern come to it. Which was not an unusual emotion for the Providence lawman to harbour—unless it was for Adam Steele.

'You really do look pretty damn sick, Steele.'

'That's what I said, Len,' Harlan Grout reminded.

'So I reckon I must look as lousy as I feel,' the Virginian answered thickly, raised a gloved hand to explore his face: felt a swelling on his jaw, a smaller one above his right eye.

'Not just those bumps,' Huey Attrill told him. 'Your colour's off. And you're eyes look like——'

'But I reckon I'm alive,' Steele cut in flatly. Held off from rubbing the right side of his belly. Where the pain was sharpest and there was an uncomfortable moist feeling he had already discovered was not caused by external bleeding. He resisted the temptation, also, to groan that anyway he'd be likely to stay alive if nothing vital was ruptured, seeping blood into parts of his body it was not supposed to be. Instead he gestured toward the kid and his would-be executioner, said: 'Better chance of that than Clavell, anyway.'

'And Taggart if he starts the horse to a bolt,' Fallows promised with low-voiced determination. 'If he does that and I don't kill him here, I'll see to it he stands trial for murder and——'

'There you go, Jethro!' Ryan called down from his perch at the top of the pole. 'All connected. You wanna try her out?'

O'Mally dry washed his hands, rubbed them down the sides of his pants, like it was a humid day of high summer and his palms were sticky with sweat.

'It's a friggin' trick, I tell you.' Lacy rasped. Made to swing away. 'Let's beat it, Bud!'

But the commanding glance he directed at the blond-haired man was unseen by him. For Bud gazed with the same fixed intensity as everyone else at where O'Mally shifted from a squat into a kneeling attitude, set down his pipe on the ground beside him, began to work the telegraph key. Fast, but not sure. He stopped suddenly, muttered a curse under his breath, withdrew his hand, wiped it. Looked around at his eager audience, up at Ryan, admitted:

'Guess I'm a little nervous. Sorry.'

'Take it easy, pal,' Ryan called down. 'Ain't nobody gettin' charged for the time we use the line.'

O'Mally started again, his hand moving at a markedly slower rate, a look of deep concentration on his fleshy face. Until he got into his stride, speeded up to a cadence with the key he was obviously used to. He showed his near toothless gums in a broad grin.

After several seconds while he had been as caught up as

everyone else in the drama of transmitting the message, Fallows rasped to Steele:

'If Taggart gets to stand trial, he won't be alone. There's plenty of accessories before the fact. And I'm not so sure you——'

'Just the one crime has been committed as of now, Len,' Attrill pointed out. 'And we're about to find out if the guilty party is among us.'

The newspaperman was usually not the most forceful of men outside the editorial comment column of the Providence *Post-Despatch*: and invariably he was either firmly on the side of the sheriff or he took no stand at all.

Silence, disturbed only by river sounds, followed the ending of the transmission.

'It ain't friggin' gonna work!' Bud complained, sounded as disappointed as most of the others looked.

'Well?' Taggart asked. His hand above the mare's rump started to shudder.

'Pete?' O'Mally called to the man held at the top of the pole by a leather sling and spiked boots.

'Mr Ryan?' Davy Clavell's voice sounded like the rope was already tight around his neck, constricting his throat, making it almost impossible for him to force out the words.

Because these were the first coherent words the boy had spoken in a long time, many heads were swung toward him. He was seen to be staring up at Ryan who, after checking on the hook-up of the wire from the key to the overhead line, glanced from O'Mally to Clavell and back again. On his face was a look of helplessness not often seen there. He promised:

'It's connected up right! I don't know! Maybe they haven't got the line into——'

'They must've by now!' O'Mally cut in.

'There could be a fault!' Clavell's voice was strident, his suddenly scarlet face above the rope noose expressing desperation. 'We didn't check the line all the way——'

'They're friggin' stallin', Taggart!' Lacy snarled. 'The kid's one of their own, ain't he? They'll try anythin' to——'

Ryan urged: 'Try to raise them again, Jethro!'

'Yeah, do that!' Fallows ordered. Shot a scowling glance at

Taggart. 'You'll wait, mister?'

Steele felt drained. He was fearfully certain something vital had been injured and was leaking blood, maybe poison, through his insides. He would either pass out, or be sick. But he forced himself to ignore this conviction something was seriously wrong with him. Which did not help any to ease the hurting, but at least enabled him to concentrate on what was happening around him. And he fixed it in his mind that if he was to die for his part in the day's events, he would make restitution to some extent for however much he had been to blame.

He refused to look toward his gelding, invite wishful thoughts concerning the Colt Hartford that jutted from the boot. Instead, he kept Huey Attrill on the periphery of his vision. Told himself over and over, without devoting more than an infinitesimal amount of his attention to the mental exercise, he could get to the newspaperman, wrench the Winchester from his grasp and do what had to be done.

The key began to tap out a response to O'Mally's message. He yelled:

'Hey, we're through!'

'It's a trick, I tell——'

'Shut up!' Taggart snarled at Lacy. 'Shut up, damn you!'

'Yeah, shut up, all of you!' O'Mally roared against a rising volume of excited talk from the main group of the erstwhile lynch mob. 'I gotta... Oh, shit, I ain't got no pencil and paper!'

'Here!' Attrill dug inside his coat. 'Shout the letters out!'

Steele's self-confidence increased. He felt stronger by the moment. Less concerned about what was happening inside him. Offered: 'Here, let me take that, feller.'

He grasped the barrel of the Winchester.

After a quick glance at Steele, the newspaperman said absently: 'Obliged.'

Surrendered the rifle so he had both hands free to write. Pulled a pencil and sheaf of paper from a pocket.

'*P!*' O'Mally yelled. 'Oh, shit! I missed some before that! *E-A-T-M-E-S—*'

'Repeat message... They're askin' us for a repeat, Jethro!'

Davy Clavell yelled.

'An *A* and a *G* and an *E*!' O'Mally shouted. 'Yeah, they want a repeat! That's what they want! I'll get right to it, boy! Don't you worry about that!'

Abe Steiner, then Harold Archer loped forward. The rest of the group crowded behind them along the trail, clustered around the telegraph company man as he began to operate the key faster than ever.

Attrill forced his way through, commanding the others to make way for him to take down the message. Fallows and Grout went with him.

Lacy and Bud ambled to join the throng.

So, in a few moments, Steele stood alone beside the tree. Twenty or so yards away, the boy on the horse and the man beside the animal also waited and watched in isolation.

Steele sloped Huey Attrill's Winchester to his shoulder, noted the hammer was not cocked. Clavell and Taggart seemed unaware of him, stared intently at the tense, silent crowd: from somewhere in the centre of which came the now familiar blips as Jethro O'Mally worked the telegraph key. Until the sound abruptly ceased.

O'Mally, his voice husky with excitement, hurried to explain: 'I've told them: Urgent we know girl's state of health. Can she talk? It's what Sheriff Fallows told me to say. Awhile back.'

Another stillness blanketed the crowd, the men mute and immobile with expectancy. They remained so when the reply began to sound in another series of long and short blips. Tapped out at a less frenetic speed than Jethro O'Mally by his brother Jack or Kenny Coggins: the operator at the Providence stage line depot maybe not so skilled, or working more slowly to avoid making mistakes or being misunderstood.

O'Mally's voice sang out clearly now, as he called each letter for Huey Attrill to write down: '*G-I-R-L-S-A-Y-S-D-A-V-Y-N-O-T-O-N-E*...'

Pete Ryan at the top of the pole, and Davy Clavell on the horse, both of them experienced at hearing messages spelled out one letter at a time, began to grin their relief before the incoming transmission was over. Anticipated the final three words:

'... *W-H-O-R-A-P-E-D-H-E-R.*'

The boy mouthed something, or maybe spoke aloud words that were lost against a sudden barrage of sound: as some of the men reacted raucously to the message they deciphered. Others, less literate, stridently demanded to be told what news had been received.

'Kate Taggart's fine!' Huey Attrill announced, his voice shrill with excitement, clearly rising above the tumult. 'She said it wasn't the boy who attacked her!'

'How do we know——' Lacy started to snarl as the din began to diminish.

'My girl!' Arnie Taggart blurted, almost sobbed. Staggered into a clumsy run. Eager to get close to the telegraph key, demanded more information, his mind filled with just a single image. 'Ask them if Kate's——'

Some of those who saw the danger yelled at him.

He banged into the horse.

The docile mare, already made skittish by sudden noise followed by silence then noise again, shied to the right.

Davy Clavell vented a scream, toppled out of the saddle.

Steele uttered a groan of despair, stepped back against the tree. Slammed the rifle stock into his shoulder. Pumped the action. Squeezed the trigger. Pumped and squeezed again. And again. Again. His shoulder started to hurt worse than any other area of his body with recoil after recoil. But anguish was a more powerful sensation than agony. For stretched seconds he was sicker in mind than body.

The focus of his attention was centred where the rope was tied around the branch. It was the only part of the rope which offered an unmoving target. The rest of it swayed and twisted with the weight of the boy, jerking and writhing as he struggled vainly to wrench free of the stranglehold.

On the periphery of his vision, though, the Virginian was vividly aware of Taggart. The rancher seemed to be rooted to the spot by horror while he stared helplessly at the wriggling, squirming, kicking form gruesomely suspended in mid air.

Then, while Steele maintained the barrage of gunfire, black

powder smoke drifted, expended shellcases spun high in the air. Taggart lunged toward the boy, his good arm curled out in front of him. He hooked this around the kicking legs; sought to trap them and support Clavell's weight.

An instant later the knot blasted apart, the body of the boy became a weight too heavy to bear in his killer's one-arm grip. Taggart overbalanced, but refused to relinquish his burden. So fell heavily to the hard-packed dirt of the trail with Davy Clavell.

The man sobbed, the boy was silent.

Steele felt he had never been so strong in his life. Nor so savagely angry. He emptied the repeater: the final three bullets uselessly exploding bark fragments and rope fibres. He pumped the action, squeezed the trigger of the emptied rifle: three, four, maybe five times before he realised the futility of what he was doing.

His rage diminished.

He became aware that once more just the moving water sounds of the river held silence at bay. He felt he was going to gag on the acrid taste of gunsmoke. Was sure if he did get sick to his stomach it would be a crimson stained mess that erupted out of him.

The prospect of submerging himself in the river was suddenly tantalisingly attractive.

Off to one side, the mare whinnied. From elsewhere the gelding responded with a snort.

Unaware he had become the centre of stunned attention, Steele hurled away the empty Winchester, voided his mind of inconsequential images. Walked slowly to where Davy Clavell lay utterly still: Arnie Taggart was starting to get to his feet beside the inert form.

'Steele!' Len Fallows forced from his fear tightened throat.

Taggart began to explain: 'Mister, I was tryin' to . . .'

Steele, impassive faced, did not even glance at the shocked rancher. He pushed out an arm, moved it slowly to the side. Did not quite touch the pale, haggard faced Taggart. For the man responded like an automaton to the gesture, stepped out of the Virginian's path.

Now Steele heard the telegraph key was blipping again.

Many voices talking. Not to him, though, and he felt a mild sense of gratitude nobody was asking anything of him. For he was still worried he would not be able to speak without triggering nausea.

Beside the boy, he dropped on to his haunches. Rolled Clavell over on to his back and had everybody's first impression confirmed. The kid was dead. Tongue stuck out of his gaping mouth, the so-blue eyes bulged wide, the skin an unnatural colour.

In Steele's hunkered-down attitude, the outside seam of his right pants leg gaped. So it was easy to reach through the slit, draw the knife from the boot sheath.

'Steele!' a voice commanded.

He guessed it was Fallows. The sheriff said nothing more as the Virginian first cut free the hanging rope, then that around the wrists of the dead boy. Loosened the slip knot, pulled the noose from around the darkened, rope-burned neck.

'Hey now, Arnie, don't you fret none until you know you have to,' Charlie Lacy called sneeringly.

'Yeah, there's only these telegraph company guys who claim——' Bud began to agree, with less conviction.

A fast-rising volume of talk angrily denied the men's implication. Until abruptly all voices were stilled once more. Attention swung back toward Steele beside the corpse. Drawn there as the Virginian slowly came erect, turned around to look toward the men, the knife still clutched in his gloved hand.

'Steele!' Fallows snarled hoarsely once more, elbowed his way clear of the press of men. His Frontier Colt was levelled at the Virginian. Then he seemed to dry up, lost the ability to speak.

Taggart had backed off to a point midway between Steele and the men. He showed an expression that pleaded for understanding.

'Honest, mister! I know I should've . . . My little girl! She's all I've got!'

'You've got nothin' I want, feller.'

Fallows warned: 'Steele, don't do anything stupid!'

Taggart pleaded: 'I just want to go to my girl.'

'Steele!'

'Take it easy, Sheriff,' the Virginian drawled. Stooped to return the knife to the boot sheath. Turned toward the mare, took up the reins. Added in a sardonic tone that revealed nothing of his simmering anger because of what happened to Clavell, nor the degree of physical pain he endured: 'The boy never was anything to me. I've come for my horse.'

13

At Jethro O'Mally's request the Virginian consented to have his mare, the only spare horse, transport the body of Davy Clavell back to town. But he did not wait around to take any part in completing the business at the bend in the river where the water rushed out of the gorge and boiled white through the rocks.

He set off alone astride the gelding. Because alone was how he mostly liked to be. Alone was certainly how he liked to be when he was hurting so badly as he did this late afternoon on the brink of evening.

He hurt physically so much he was still concerned over whether he would survive the cause of the sharp pain floating in liquid that was sometimes concentrated in the lower right of his belly, at others shot flares of burning sensation through his entire abdomen.

A bad conscience also bothered him and he was trying to come to terms with this when he heard a rider approaching from behind.

He did not turn to see who it was until the newcomer slowed his mount, came up alongside him, matched the pace of his horse to that of the gelding. Spoke.

'Steele?'

Because of the man's thick beard and element-burnished skin, Jake Lineker's face was little more than a dark smudge against the gloom: for the sun had by now dipped behind the ridge on the south western flank of the valley. But the tone of the single syllable conveyed his dejection.

'Something?' Steele asked, sensed that the man was

looking hard at him, so pre-empted the query. 'I don't look any worse than I feel, feller.'

For awhile it seemed like the tenant farmer who worked Josh Marley's land to the east of town was about to pursue the point. But he confined himself to:

'So I figure the last thing you wanna hear is other folk's troubles?'

'Could help me keep my mind off my own. Self-pity's not the best kind of food for thought.'

'I ain't . . .' Lineker started to bristle, but realised he had misunderstood the Virginian's meaning. Cleared his throat. 'I can say some things to you and you won't——'

'Go ahead,' Steele invited, needed to speak to check a groan. Turned his head away, hid a grimace of pain.

The man who for so long had held a grudge against the Virginian said quickly: 'I'm one crazy sonofabitch or worse to have gotten myself mixed up in what's happened, Steele.'

He seemed relieved to have made the admission, until the response came:

'Reckon we have that in common, feller.'

In a much more familiar tone, the man who might conceivably have been Steele's father-in-law groaned: 'What we ain't got in common is how you can make light of when things go bad, mister.' The sour tone implied irritable criticism of this aspect of the Virginian's character.

Steele told him grimly: 'It was you chose to ride with me. If you don't like the company, the remedy for what ails you is real easy to swallow, I reckon?'

Lineker took a little time to reflect, but not to weigh up the alternatives Steele offered him. He simply organised in his mind what he wanted to say. Admitted: 'Ridin' to catch you up, I had everythin' set: what I was gonna say.'

Steele's tone was triggered by impatience with Jake Lineker's beating about the bush. He prompted him as a snarl: 'Last time you rode with a lynch mob, you were top hand. And it was my neck you planned to put in the noose.'

'Yeah, but——'

'You thought you had good reason then?'

'Sure I did!'

'And this time the same?'

Lineker was disconcerted, almost used anger to mask his uncertainty. Then he compressed his lips within the dark beard. Next blurted: 'Some of the others asked me. Tell you the same goes for them. Abe and Archer. Mike Morrison. Marty Dyer. All of them feel the same, I guess. Except for Charlie Lacy, that hard-nosed, mean-hearted sonofa——'

'Why tell me, feller?'

'What?'

'Why does it have to be my ear you and the rest of the bleeding hearts want to bend?'

The beefily built man again needed to make a conscious effort to check his temper. He took a deep breath before he replied: 'Because we figure it wasn't true what you said. About the kid meanin' nothin' to you. It was plain. Way you acted from the start. Way you tried to stop Taggart—us all—from stringin' him up.'

'You're wrong, feller.'

'So what was it all about?' Lineker jerked a thumb over his shoulder. Then peered back along the night shrouded trail. Another rider was heard approaching from the north, at a canter.

'It was me doing something I thought I had good reason for, feller. That's what it was.'

'It's Harlan Grout,' Lineker announced as the rider closed with them, slowed his mount. Then the farmer called to the liveryman: 'I ain't sure I'm gettin' through to him.'

Grout came up on the other side of Steele and the Virginian felt irritated there was now nowhere he could look should he need to hide grimaces of pain.

'What?' Grout asked absently, did not sound interested in hearing a reply.

'I'm just tryin' to get it across to Steele . . . Some of us acted clear out of our minds after Arnie Taggart and Len Fallows brought the girl in this mornin'.'

Grout nodded, still seemed indifferent to the subject. But allowed: 'I guess with what happened to your own daughter, Mr Lineker, you at least can be forgiven for——'

'I ain't askin' no forgiveness!' the thickly-bearded farmer

snapped. 'Don't figure none of us want that from no one. Except God. But Steele, the way he always seems to get things right while the rest of us are——'

Now Grout, stockily built, running to fat, and ruddy complexioned, felt he could make a useful contribution to the talk. Shook his head as he growled: 'If you hear what Len Fallows has to say about that, Steele didn't get nothin' right this time.' He fixed the Virginian with a level, quizzical gaze. 'Len reckons if it hadn't been for you, the kid'd still be alive. Safe and sound in the lock-up until Kate Taggart come to and said her piece. He figures as how you had the boy hid at Trail's End when the posse was there. Reason you wouldn't join up with us. Then you and him rode together. Until you had some kinda bust up—seein' as how he run into the lynchers before you did.'

Steele was aware of them closely studying each profile of his face. Was struck by the notion that if he now grimaced at a stab of pain, they would think he expressed his anguish over what had happened. Eventually, he said flatly:

'Fallows is a better lawman that he's most times given credit for.'

'You mean that really is what happened, Mr Steele? Grout asked, surprised, his interest deepening.

'Close enough.'

'The kid was out at your place when we come there?'

'Right?'

'And you were helpin' him to get away?'

'Just from Providence, feller. We were making for Broadwater. We both reckoned he'd be safer with the sheriff there than back in the Providence lock-up. The way Taggart was rallying support.'

'Why did he ride hell-for-leather away from you, before we stopped him in his tracks?' Lineker asked.

'He decided I was taking him to Broadwater for the wrong reason,' Steele answered.

'Uh?'

'It didn't matter to me if he was guilty or innocent, feller. I wasn't taking him up there so much to stop him getting lynched.'

'What?'

'It was more the other way around.'

'I still don't know what the hell you're talkin' about,' Lineker complained.

'I think maybe I'm startin' to,' Grout said thoughtfully, his face deeply lined by a frown. 'It was the lynch mob you was protectin', not the kid?'

'But that's crazy!' Lineker snarled.

Grout countered, peering across the front of the Virginian at the farmer: 'You and the rest of Taggart's bunch were the crazy ones. And if there were enough of you, them of us with Len Fallows would've been crazy to try to stop you bustin' the kid outta the town lock-up if he was there. Stringin' him up.'

After several moments thought, Lineker shook his head. Did a double-take at Steele and admitted: 'That's too damn deep for me. Unless . . .' He shook his head again. 'No, Steele ain't the kind to care about the likes of us. I've said my piece, spoke up for some of the others who feel bad as me about what happened to that poor kid. Gonna get back to Ellie now. She'll be worried about me.'

He thudded in his heels, was soon racing away down the trail through the timbered valley which showed white in moonlight. When the pounding of hooves had diminished in the distance, Harlan Grout seemed embarrassed. He was on the brink of speaking several times before he finally said:

'I got to admit it, Mr Steele. It kinda don't sound right to me, either. You goin' to so much trouble on account of other folks. A lot of them who don't give too much of a shit about you, even?'

'It turned out not to be right, feller.'

'What?'

'It was wrong. From the start. But then nobody can be right all the time, uh?'

Grout thought about this, then shook his head, defeated. 'You lost me, Mr Steele. Boy, do I need a drink. So much, it's startin' to hurt. I'll see you around.'

He took off in the wake of Jake Lineker. And while the clattering of his mount's hooves was still loud in the quiet night, Steele clutched at the area of his abdomen where the pain was now centred. Growled through teeth clenched in a grimace: 'Sure wish the medicine for what ails me was so easy to come by.'

14

Steele had just one positive thought during the remainder of the ride that night. This when he reached the point where the spur cut off the main trail, forded the Providence River to follow Timber Creek up to Trail's End.

In a thousand situations there would have been no need to consider a decision. A man like Steele, with a home like Trail's End to go to, went home. Without a home, a man like Steele who was wounded, went somewhere he could be by himself. Endure his hurt alone. Away from prying eyes. Away from those who might take advantage of his hurting to settle old scores.

Steele rode on by the Timber Creek spur with just a passing thought, a sidelong glance up the night-shrouded, timber-clad slope beyond the ford.

This injury was of a kind he instinctively knew he could not handle on his own. He had been hurt before: maybe not as often as he deserved. But never had it been like this. The gun, the boot, the fist or the head had struck him at such an angle with such force on some vital part of his anatomy that the damage it caused was not going to be healed just by time and rest alone.

Maybe even Thadius Mackay, the local doctor who at least knew his limitations, would not be able to mend him. But Doc Mackay was the best chance he had in the valley tonight.

Like earlier Steele had been the best chance there was for Davy Clavell. The kid had thought so, anyway: at first.

Mistakes happened. Like he told Harlan Grout, nobody was right all the time. A man could but try to do what he thought was right. Just as the men who rode with the revenge-bent Arnie Taggart had thought they were right.

He cursed aloud in the quiet darkness.

That was not the line of thought on which he wanted to keep a grip as he struggled to stay awake, to remain in the saddle. And he forced himself to return to the question of if it was crazy to die for a cause.

Not the Southern Cause, all those years ago. The rights or wrongs of that were now purely academic. More recently: the cause of Davy Clavell's life. Tied to this the peace of mind of a bunch of basically decent but temporarily unbalanced men. Who conspired to commit an act they would surely regret the rest of their lives.

If he were to die because of this, it would now be for a lost cause.

Would a better reason to die be the protection of a piece of California dirt called Trail's End? Or would that be just as stupid?

No, he decided: tried to shake his head but could not do so. If he had to put his life on the line for a cause, Trail's End was worth it. He didn't have any papers to grant him legal title to the land, but to his way of thinking it was his by right after so long. In truth, outside of his life and the Colt Hartford rifle bequeathed him by his father, it was all he possessed that he cared about. It had to be worth dying for.

But, he had evidently come to accept without realising the conclusion he reached, the Trail's End spread was just a part of a whole lot more.

The *valley* in which it was set.

The *town* in the valley.

Damnit, the *people* of the town and of the valley!

The kid was dead. An innocent kid. Killed by a kind of cruel accident, maybe, but nonetheless killed by those Providence River Valley people who now had to live with the knowledge of what they had taken part in.

Steele had given it his best shot, tried to avert the tragedy. And made the wrong decision. But for the right reason. So if he was going to recover from what hurt him so badly at least he should not have to live the remainder of his life with any kind of regret.

'It's Steele!' a man rasped.

A woman pleaded: 'Oh, yes: he can stop this, surely?'

Steele instinctively reined in his horse, had to struggle to raise his chin up from his chest. Not until then had he known that was where it rested while emotional anguish negated physical pain. Now he was gripped by a groundless fear that for many stretched seconds swamped the hurt. Hot sweat oozed through the surface of his skin and he felt like he had just shuddered awake from a nightmare.

Then reality turned the beads of sweat to particles of ice. Partly because of the chill night air, partly because he briefly glimpsed component areas of the scene spread before him. His vision blurred at first.

He had halted the gelding on the end of the north trail, where it emerged at the town square between the meeting hall and the law office. As his vision cleared and he began to register more firmly what he saw, he ran a gloved hand down the neck of the gelding which had carried him so far without guidance. While he, if he had not fallen asleep during the ride, had at times sunk into a depth of detachment just one step removed.

'Adam, you look——'

He glanced to the right. Saw it was Lavinia Attwood who addressed him in shocked tones. Knew he should have guessed this, for the spinster schoolma'am was the only person in the valley who used his given name: since Susannah Lineker was killed.

He saw she was one of a dozen or so people gathered out front of the meeting hall. Bathed by the glow of the near full moon and a wedge of lamplight which shafted out from the open doorway of the building. Because the hall was lit, he guessed the group had earlier congregated inside.

He felt exhausted, but no longer had pain in any part of his body. This worried him. Especially because he did not have that burning sensation in his belly. Nobody as badly hurt as he had been got cured so quickly. Thus, he was numb and he thought this was a bad sign.

His voice sounded hollow to his own ears when he said: 'I guess now I look a whole lot worse than I feel. That's bad.'

The schoolteacher with the piercing eyes peered at him long and hard. He saw deep concern on her sharp-featured, lightly-powdered face. Glanced fleetingly at the others in the group, felt sure he recognised all the faces. So they were townspeople, and he should be able to name every face. But he had no inclination to put his mind to this.

More importantly, he had no wish to see such anxiety on the face of the woman who had proved to be one of his few true and tried friends since he first rode into the Providence River Valley.

Joanne Morrison—Michael's mother, he recalled—was in the group. This came to him as soon as he turned his head away from them. Along with the banker, Ethan Brady. He it was who had called Steele's name, to jerk him out from near sleep. It was the homely Faith Kenway who claimed the Virginian could stop something. The widow who ran the hardware store. Cut hair in a room out back of the store. Was reputed to possess second sight. Roland Decker, the town butcher who had such a low opinion of Adam Steele, was there. And his wife, Amelia...

Steele's attention was drawn to the north east corner of the town square. And what he saw there, vividly clear, acted to stem the flood of inconsequential names to match with familiar faces that came unbidden into his mind.

Between the stage line depot and the Golden Gate Saloon the two would-be undertakers who came to town this morning would shortly be in need of undertaking services themselves. Unless somebody was more successful at stopping a double lynching than Steele had been in saving the neck of Davy Clavell.

'It was the one named Pope who did those terrible things to Kate Taggart,' Lavinia Attwood started to explain in a doom-laden voice. 'When the unfortunate child recovered some of her senses, she remained delirious with the shock of what happened to her. It was only after extensive questioning the child was able to reveal the boy her father accused of the crime was not responsible.'

'It came over the new wire that the news was despatched too late to save that poor young man.' This from Joanne Morrison, in whose premises the Providence telegraph office had been established.

There was a telegraph pole in the gap between the saloon and the stage line depot, rising to almost twice the height of the roofs of the single story flanking buildings. Backed up to the pole was the flatbed wagon with a two horse team in the traces aboard which Cole Pope and Albert Dean had ridden into town this morning.

Now they stood, side by side, on the very back of the wagon. Hands tied between them. Forced to remain rigidly erect because their heads were through the noose ends of ropes that were fixed to the top of the pole.

'Then a woman with a child arrived in Providence, Adam,' Lavinia Attwood took up the account.

'Mrs Pope and her son,' Steele murmured absently without turning his head away from the corner of the square where two men awaited imminent death. 'I see their buckboard outside the boarding house.'

'Yes. They're staying at Blanche's place. The woman said she'd met men on the trail from Broadwater. Knew a young girl had been attacked.'

It was the rangy, grey-moustached Kenny Coggins who had fixed the ropes to the top of the pole. The leather strap which had been slung around his waist while he worked was now draped over a shoulder. He was stooped down, to unfasten the iron spikes from beneath his boots.

'She's a fine woman, that Mrs Pope,' Faith Kenway said. 'Asked about the child who'd been attacked. Said she'd like to see her.'

The barrel-bodied Jack O'Mally was up on the bed of the wagon. He it was, apparently, who had used his so strangely delicate hands to drop the nooses over the heads of the condemned men, tighten them.

'Pope and Dean had left town by then, of course,' Roland

Decker took up the story. 'South. Took off soon as they found out the Taggart girl wasn't dead from gettin' hit over the head, we figure. Seems that's the way Pope likes to . . . The woman . . . The person . . . His victim, she has to be uncon——'

'I'm certain Adam has no wish to hear every grim detail, Mr Decker!' Miss Attwood cut in caustically.

'No, Roland, I'm sure, too,' Amelia Decker agreed.

The scene of the hanging was brightly illuminated by the moon augmented with lamplight that spilled out of the window and batwinged doorway of the saloon. This lamplight cast men's shadows, which moved a little every now and then, as the watchers in the Golden Gate sipped their drinks while they waited for the final act of the grisly tableau.

'The Pope woman guessed from the first time she heard about Kate Taggart,' Faith Kenway said dejectedly. 'Guessed it was her husband who——'

Amelia Decker cut in bitterly: 'If she'd told Mr Taggart and the others about it, that poor boy would still be alive.'

'My God, woman, she is married to the man and——' the Widow Kenway countered irritably.

Lavinia Attwood cut in: 'You see, Adam, it has happened before. In Kansas where the Popes lived. He raped a woman there and would have been arrested or worse had he not run away. His poor wife and son were hounded out of town by their neighbours.'

'They still deserve a fair and proper trial!' Ethan Brady insisted.

'Isn't that what we all met up here to agree on?' Roland Decker countered irritably.

'If she acted wrongly at the start, she did the right thing eventually, Adam,' Lavinia Attwood said, cut across a murmuring of discontent. She used a tone of voice more usually reserved for forestalling disobedience in the schoolhouse. 'After she saw the Taggart girl—the state the poor child was in—Mrs Pope named her husband.'

Steele allowed his thoughts to be sidetracked by the fact that Thadius Mackay's buggy was not on the square. The fat medical man went everywhere in his phaeton. The Virginian wondered if he could make it to the doctor's house in the timber without passing out.

'What she said spread like wildfire, of course,' the schoolteacher went on. 'And it was not long before every soul in Providence heard the truth of what happened to Kate Taggart.

'The two men with the telegraph company, Mr O'Mally and Mr Coggins, immediately downed tools. Set off in pursuit of Pope and Dean. As you see, Adam, they found them!'

'There's some folks hoped they wouldn't bring the culprits back to Providence,' Brady revealed in hushed tones. 'Hoped they'd deal with them out of town.'

'Others of us feel strongly the men must stand trial in a court of law,' Miss Attwood insisted. 'Of course they had to be brought back to Providence! At first everyone did the right and proper thing. The men admitted their guilt and were locked in——'

'It's the tall, skinny one did it to the girl,' Decker said. 'The other one, he just didn't say anythin' about it, so we——'

Ethan Brady snapped: 'In law, they're both equally responsible.'

'They were confined in the lock-up and the final work of bringing the telegraph line to the stage depot was finished,' Lavinia Attwood took up the telling of events again. 'Almost at the very moment this was completed, a message was received.

'Mr O'Mally had time to answer it, say the boy did not hurt the girl. But not to add that the true attacker had been apprehended before another message came in. To say the poor boy had been hanged.'

'Then Mr O'Mally sent another message,' Joanne Morrison said. 'We're certain that even if he didn't lie, he didn't tell the whole truth.'

Steele supplied absently: 'Something about the girl not knowing the man who attacked her, as I recall.'

'Precisely,' the schoolteacher said. 'Which was true, but not the whole truth!'

'Then those two took the law into their own hands,' Roland

Decker growled.

'And wasn't too many men hereabouts eager to try to stop them,' Faith Kenway countered pointedly.

Except for the north east corner and where the north trail ended, the square was unnaturally quiet for this early evening hour. So quiet it was possible to hear a sound of weeping from within the Knight boarding house. But whether a child spilled tears of terror, or a woman of remorse, it was not possible to discern.

Then, from far to the north came the muted by distance clatter of many cantering hooves: a large group of riders returning with heavy hearts, some guilty consciences and the corpse of Davy Clavell.

Steele knew the men directly involved in the double lynching were aware of his return to town. He was just as certain that they did not take their time over the final preprarations in order that the newcomer should be fully informed of events during his absence.

Now, as Jack O'Mally climbed wearily down off the wagon, went to one of the team horses, Coggins to the other, they both looked across at the Virginian sitting the gelding against the backdrop of anxious townspeople illuminated by the meeting hall light.

The older, heavier man, his fleshy face set with a grim frown, called: 'We got it over the wire, Steele! And a guy named Lineker then the local liveryman gave us the news first hand! Davy's dead for somethin' he didn't do, right?'

Pope shuddered, Dean vented a despairing groan.

Steele looked from the self-confessed rapist to the accessory alongside him, who maybe now was not so sure he had been right to stand by his friend in another sense.

Then at the shadows cast by the watchers in the saloon. Men who, right or wrong, did not intend to interfere.

Glanced around the quiet square. Knew people were inside some of the buildings on three sides of it. And in others, scattered throughout the town in the timber. People who considered it right, for whatever reason, not to get involved.

The citizens of Providence who had gathered in the meeting hall to discusss what to do, unable to reach a decision: except that it was right not to act on their own account.

The impassive expression on the bristled face of the Virginian showed nothing of what he was thinking: nor hinted at his pain and anxiety about it as he listened to the thudding of hooves out on the north trail. Where a group of more committed men would likely be undecided if they knew the present situation here.

Except for Arnie Taggart, who would surely be convinced of what was right. As would Len Fallows, his conviction diametrically opposed.

A few of these people Steele's friends: all of them his neighbours.

All of them, he decided as he looked back at the two strangers about to lynch two other strangers, could make up their own damn minds about rights and wrongs now. And in the future, too: the way he was feeling.

He clutched a gloved hand at his abdomen when a sharp pain exploded there, groaned: 'Right.'

'What's that?' O'Mally called.

The word had been loud in Steele's own head. But he guessed that maybe this was because it had bounced off his teeth clenched tightly against the pain, resounded stridently around his skull.

Coggins growled: 'He said right, Jack.'

There was nothing accidental about the way the two horses in the traces of the flatbed were urged into an abrupt movement.

A word was rasped by O'Mally to Coggins. Both men put a hand to the bridle of a horse, snapped commands to the animals, lunged forward.

Just a few paces was all that were necessary: for the silent Cole Pope and the sobbing Albert Dean to have the support of the wagon jerked out from under their feet.

And they dropped a matter of inches to stretch the lynch ropes taut.

Then the only sounds made by both men as their executioners brought the horses and wagon to a silent standstill were the thuds of their writhing bodies against the telegraph pole between them.

Within moments, these sounds were ended, the men dead. Hanging suspended in limp inertia.

The hoofbeats out on the north trail rose in volume. But not so loud the gasps, cries and growls of shock, disappointment, relief and maybe even some sadistic pleasure were masked.

When the clatter of the hooves came close enough to blanket all sounds except for those from nearby, Lavinia Attwood said frostily to Steele as the Virginian turned to look at her:

'I suppose you have good reason of your own for not taking a hand in this, Adam?'

Steele's vision blurred. He felt himself sway, then start to fall. Said—or perhaps only thought he said—against another barrage of shocked voices responding to the sight of him toppling out of the saddle: 'And for taking a hand in all the . . .

. . . REST.'*

* *Which is what Adam Steele will take until the next book in the series.*